VENDETTA

Also by Ed Gorman
in Large Print:

The Day the Music Died
Wake Up Little Susie
Will You Still Love Me Tomorrow?
Ghost Town

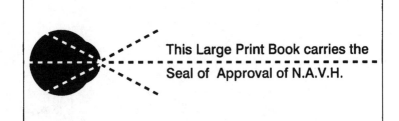

This Large Print Book carries the
Seal of Approval of N.A.V.H.

VENDETTA

Ed Gorman

Thorndike Press • Waterville, Maine

Published in 2002 by arrangement with The Berkley Publishing Group, a member of Penguin Putnam, Inc.

Thorndike Press Large Print Western Series.

The tree indicium is a trademark of Thorndike Press.

The text of this Large Print edition is unabridged. Other aspects of the book may vary from the original edition.

Cover design by Thorndike Press Staff.

Set in 16 pt. Plantin by Minnie B. Raven.

Printed in the United States on permanent paper.

Library of Congress Cataloging-in-Publication Data

Gorman, Edward.
    Vendetta / Ed Gorman.
      p. cm.
    ISBN 0-7862-3993-X (lg. print : hc : alk. paper)
    1. Large type books.   I. Title.
PS3557.O759 V46 2002
  813'.54—dc21   2002022574

To Kathy and Steve Cook

We all play many roles in life.
Each of us is somebody's hero and
somebody's villain.
— EG

PART ONE

ONE

As a little girl, Joan Grieves had had a crush on Father Peter Madsen. She knew this was wrong — the handsome padre was given to Christ and not the flesh — but she couldn't help herself.

Though the crush had faded because she was now twenty-two and knew better, Joan still turned to the padre when trouble came. And trouble had come indeed. Her father had made up his mind and there would be no changing it. He was that sort of man.

Joan moved as quickly as possible through the punishing heat of the Arizona afternoon. She wore a light blue dress stained in several places with sweat. Her blond hair was wet, too, from the heat. Her freckled, pretty face gazed blue-eyed at the saguaro cactus standing to the west of the adobe mission where Father Madsen lived. The cactus, like all else in the high desert, seemed to droop under the assault of the sun. Dogs and cats lay sprawled in the shade; horses looked as if the sun had robbed them of all spirit and purpose. The people at siesta looked so exhausted they resembled corpses. Even the children had been lashed into indolence by the searing day. Who could play in such fire?

Rosita, the ample Mexican woman who seemed to work twenty-four hours a day at the mission, smiled when she saw Joan. Rosita had helped Father Madsen take care of Joan all the time Noah had been in prison. Joan had lived at the New Mexico mission and seldom ventured into the nearby town. She had come to fear the whispers and smirks of the townspeople. They hurt far more than fists ever could.

Despite the heat, Rosita gave Joan one of her bear-hug embraces. Joan usually joked that someday Rosita would break one of Joan's ribs embracing her. But not today. Joan was beyond jokes today.

"Is Father Madsen in?" Joan said.

They stood in the tiled courtyard of the Spanish mission. The hundred-year-old mission was in bad repair these days. As the nearby town grew, the locals had found themselves less and less dependent on the order and structure the mission had given their lives. Once, it had been the central meeting place for the entire area. Children were born here, baptized here; and old folks buried here in the cemetery out back. And everybody had been eager to help the various priests who'd overseen the place keep it in good repair. But no longer. The growing town offered too many distractions.

"In the church. Saying his prayers." Rosita, a good and wise woman, carefully studied Joan's face. "Things are not so good."

"Not so good at all, Rosita. That's why I need to talk to Father Madsen."

Rosita smiled. "He will be glad to see you. The daughter he never had, as he always says." She had once confided that she too had had a crush on the priest. She sensed that sometimes his vow of celibacy was difficult to maintain. She saw the melancholy way he watched the young women at the mission dances on holy days. Rosita, whose own husband died long ago fighting Apaches, dreamed that when she reached heaven, Father Madsen would join her and they would be married. If the Good Lord permitted such couplings up there.

The church was lost to deep shadows and the scent of incense. A High Mass of some kind this morning, apparently. Incense was never used at Low Mass. In its primitive way, the church was beautiful. Nearly every part of it was wood but the statuary. No fancy marbling. No gold. No silver fretting. Just the simple but profound expression of faith stated in wood because that was all the natives could afford. Even the statue of Christ above the tabernacle was made of wood. Two long, wide rows of wooden pews. And the stations of the cross — in intricately carved wood — on both facing walls.

Father Madsen knelt at the communion rail, his hands folded, his head bowed. He wore a blue work shirt, jeans, and riding boots. Part of his job was to run the small ranch one of the wealthy townspeople had willed the mission. He had help, of course, but it was easy to see that the priest enjoyed wearing his cowhand clothes and riding his big gray. Even a priest wanted to be part of the Western myth.

When he heard her, he looked up and smiled. His hair was white now, but his face was hard and tight, heroic in the jut of nose and jaw and clarity of blue eye; he still had that almost ferocious handsomeness.

He looked away, then, bowed his head

briefly, finished his prayers (she could see his lips moving silently), then blessed himself and stood up.

Her second hug for the morning. She was glad to be lost in his powerful arms. He was six-three and was always giving youngsters lessons in boxing. Some of the rowdy young men on Friday nights liked to fight with other groups of rowdy young men. When things got too much for the sheriff and his two deputies — long drunken holiday weekends were especially tough on the lawmen — they always asked Father Madsen to help them. There wasn't a rowdy young man yet who could take him.

"Would you like to sit down?"

"Yes, Father."

"You don't look so good, my friend."

She liked when he called her "my friend." She'd never heard him call anybody else that. He'd been using it with her since she was fourteen, the year her father was sent to prison.

They sat in the front pew. As they talked, she looked up at the statue of the Virgin above the dancing red-blue-green flames of the votive candles. It was so easy to give in to despair, even when you knew that the Virgin was watching over you.

"It's Noah," the priest said.

"Yes."

"He's going after Rattigan?"

"Yes."

The priest sighed. "I'm not sure I can talk him out of it, Joan. He's a very stubborn man. One time he got mad at me — we were probably eight or something like that — and he said he wouldn't speak to me for a month. We were orphans together. We lived in the same house. How could you not speak to somebody you saw day and night seven days a week?"

She laughed softly. "But he didn't speak to you."

"It was as if he willed me out of existence. I'd look right at him and half-shout in his face, and he'd just turn away as if I wasn't even there." He laughed. "I have to admit, I was pretty impressed."

They sat and stared at the altar for a time. Laughter had left them.

"He'll get himself killed," Joan said.

"I'm not sure he cares. He just wants to get even with Rattigan. And there — I have to admit — I can't blame him. I'd want to get even, too!"

He's forty-three years old. He should have a good life ahead of him. He has to forget what happened."

The cleric sighed again. "I'll go talk to him. You know where he is?"

"That dry creek bed behind the cabin where we're staying. He's using that old Navy Colt for shooting practice."

The priest's laughter filled the church. "My Lord, that father of yours is the worst shot in this whole Territory. And target practice won't help him any, either."

She couldn't help but laugh, too. "I hope you'll tell him that, Father."

It looked pretty good, just the way the heroes of the dime novels did it. The tall, slim, dark-haired man had lined up six tin cans atop a large boulder. The cans gleamed in the scorching sunlight. The area was pure desert, sand and rock baking in the heat, empty and unmoving.

Noah looked good with the Remington .44 in his hand. The long barrel was dramatic as hell.

The trouble was, he'd fire six shots and hit only one can. One round of shots, he didn't hit even a single can. So much for being the hero of a dime novel.

Madsen watched all this from behind a pile of rocks on a hill above the dry creek bed where Noah was firing. A couple of times he smiled to himself. Couldn't help

15

it. Noah was an intelligent, hardworking, and, upon occasion, charming man. But as a gunfighter, he couldn't pour piss out of a boot.

Madsen, wearing a sombrero to protect him from the heat, ambled downhill as Noah set up the cans for another go. He'd also strapped on his holster and Colt-Frontier Six-Shooter. Madsen and Noah and Tommy Rattigan had fought the war together on the Union side. The fighting along the Mississippi, especially at Vicksburg, had shown Madsen his godless side. He had slaughtered gray soldiers without remorse. Then one night, rushing a farmhouse, he mistook a moving figure for a soldier. He fired in the darkness, only to learn that he'd killed a mother — she couldn't have been more than seventeen — and her infant son. After the war, while other men were glad to go home to their girlfriends and fiancées and wives, Madsen went directly to the seminary. He would be doing penance all his life for the terrible mistake he'd made that night.

"You hit two out of six this time, I'll give you a gold eagle."

Noah frowned. "How the hell long you been watching, Pete?"

"Long enough to know that you're

gonna be in a lot of trouble if you ever get into a gunfight."

"I'll be all right," Noah said belligerently. "You don't worry about me."

"The way I didn't worry about you when you fought Tommy Rattigan that time?"

Rattigan, Noah, and Pete had all been on the same wagon train that the Apaches attacked. They'd managed to escape, the only survivors, and had ultimately been found by a cavalry patrol and turned over to an orphanage attached to a mission on what would someday be the New Mexico border. The boys were all about the same age. Rattigan was the smartest, or at least the shrewdest. He was also the toughest. He spent his seven years — from age ten on — picking on Noah. One day Noah decided no more. He walked outside to where Rattigan was playing and blindsided him with a punch and broke his nose. At which point Rattigan gave him a beating that put him in bed for nearly a week. In the meantime Pete, who'd always been Noah's sort of informal protector, returned the favor. He put Rattigan in bed for nearly two weeks.

"This is different," Noah said, "we're grown-ups now."

"You should hear confession sometime,"

the priest said. "I don't think we ever grow up. Any of us."

Noah finished putting the last can up. He'd just finished righting it when Pete said, "Stand back, Noah."

And promptly slapped out his six-shooter and blasted away every can there.

"Still like to show off, I see."

Pete helped Noah right the cans again. "Not showing off. Just proving my point. If a middle-aged priest with not very good vision can shoot like that, what're you gonna run into when you go to face Rattigan? He'll be surrounded with gunnies as usual. And you won't stand a chance."

Noah said, "Shut up, I need to concentrate."

He concentrated and fired six times. He hit one can.

"You make me nervous is all," he said. "If you weren't here, I'd have gotten all of them." Then he grinned, the way he used to grin at Pete when they were kids.

"You stupid bastard," Pete said. "You're gonna go and get yourself killed."

Noah pretended to be shocked. "I didn't think the boys in Rome would let you talk that way."

"What the boys in Rome don't know won't hurt 'em." Pete looked up at the hill

18

where'd he'd been. Joan was there now. He waved her down. Noah saw her now, too. "You go to prison, you get out, and two months later you're leaving her again."

"I'll finish my business and then everything'll be all right."

"Oh, sure, Noah. Her mother died when she was nine in that cholera plague. And then you spend all that time in prison and she doesn't have any parent at all. And now that she's got you back, you're leaving."

Noah studied him. "You're getting good at handing out guilt."

"It's about the only thing a priest's got. Shame people into doing the right thing."

Then Joan was there. Her dress was dirty from the desert. Her fine-freckled features were glazed with sweat. She shelved a dusty hand over her eyes so she could see in the glare.

"I saw your shooting, Dad."

"I would've done a lot better except Pete here made me nervous."

"Oh, that's why you're so bad, huh?" she said.

"You two rehearse your lines in advance?" Noah said.

"We're saying this because we love you, Dad."

"You need to get on with your life, Noah."

"Oh?" For the first time, the priest had made Noah genuinely angry. "And what life would that be, Pete? I'm a convicted embezzler, remember? I should've known when Tommy Rattigan offered me a job that something was wrong. But I'd washed out as a miner and then a rancher and I didn't have much choice but to take it, did I? And all the time he was using me. He'd embezzled all that money and he needed somebody to blame it on. He knew exactly what he was doing. You remember my trial, Pete? The jury was out twenty-seven minutes. I remember the look on my attorney's face when they came back so fast. I didn't have to wait to hear the verdict. I read it on my attorney's face. I stayed real clean in prison."

Now, he included both of them. "But who's going to hire me? Would you trust a convicted embezzler? I can get a job, that's right, but what *kind* of job? Prison broke me. I don't have the strength I used to. So there isn't much manual labor I can do. And even then, everybody'll keep an eye on me. No matter where I go, I'll always be the embezzler. And I'm sorry I sound so damned sorry for myself. But it's just the way it is and you know it and I know it."

Joan didn't say anything, just slid into her father's arms and held him tight. The truth of what he'd said had silenced all three of them.

Pete looked at the tin cans lined up atop the boulder. His hand touched the butt of his Six-Shooter. He wanted to shoot a hell of a lot more than tin cans. God forgive him . . . he'd always had a genuine hatred of Tommy Rattigan, ever since they were ten years old. He was the most manipulative, cruel, and selfish person the priest had ever known. And probably ever would know.

He wanted to give his friend Noah another round of reasons for not going after Rattigan. But how could he when he'd do the same thing in Noah's place?

Joan knew it would happen. The question was when and how.

She was asleep and then not asleep. Something moving in the cabin. And then before *seeing* what — or who — was moving, she thought: This is the night when he does it. *This is the night he leaves and I'll never see him again, Lord, and I don't think he has any idea how much I love him or how much I'll miss him.* Her thoughts were a sort of prayer. Father Madsen often said that sometimes the best prayers aren't prayers at all but just thoughts we send to the Lord.

He was almost funny, the way he moved around in the cabin, trying not to make any noise, big theatrical steps like the vaudeville clowns she'd seen on her one and only trip to Phoenix that time. He didn't want to wake her. He didn't want to confront her.

And in truth, she didn't want to confront him. It had all been said, anyway. Three days and nights of arguing since that day in the dry creek bed, shooting — and missing — all those tin cans. He was a terrible shot, a clumsy man, and not an especially clever one. How in God's name was he going to confront Rattigan? But what was the use of yelling at him anymore?

So she lay there and listened. Pretended to be asleep. Tears gleamed in her eyes and she wound her rosary beads around her fingers, wound them so tight they almost cut into her, like biting her tongue so she wouldn't speak. He was filling a carpetbag. He didn't own much — you don't accumulate many worldly possessions in prison — and so packing didn't take him long at all. One thing she saw him take was the photogravure of his wife. She had seen him put it on his chest at night and lie with it all night. He'd told her once, after a night of drinking beer, that he'd done the same thing with another such photogravure when he'd been in prison. He'd said that her picture helped ward off all the evil spirits that hid in every shadow in prison.

A delicate man he wasn't, and this made her smile. He bumped into chairs, the bureau, the stove. He swore under his breath when he couldn't find something. He did everything except roll a cigarette and light it up. He would have made a terrible sneak thief.

And then he came to the cot where she slept and said, "Thanks for pretending to be asleep, honey. It'll be easier like this."

And then he bent down and kissed her. And she couldn't ever remember being kissed more tenderly, more lovingly. She knew at last, through this kiss, just how much her father *did* love her. And she also knew how devastated she would be when Rattigan destroyed him. She had no doubt about that. Father Madsen had told her too many stories about Rattigan for her to think otherwise.

"I love you, honey," he said, and she could tell that he was crying, too. So many things she heard in that lonesome voice of his just then — anger and fear and urgency (all the feelings he had about Rattigan) — and yet that odd sweetness, too, that little bit of perfect love he kept just for her, kept unsullied by all the other emotions that tormented him.

He left. Of course, he had to bump into a chair one last time for good measure, and she had to restrain herself from laughing and crying at the same time. And then he was gone and there was just the silence of the desert night.

In the morning, she rode to the mission and told Father Madsen about her father leaving. He took her to the small, crudely fashioned communion rail and they knelt next to each other as the priest led them in a rosary for Noah's safe return.

Joan found herself going to town more often than she ever had. The reason was so she could pass by the telegraph office. Quirt, the man who ran the small station, knew her by sight. She figured if he had any news for her he'd rush it out to her.

But he never had any news. Just a kind of flirtatious smile. He was a widower with a potbelly and wooden teeth, but there was a sweetness about him she liked. Nobody had ever beamed at her before with wooden teeth.

She started wearing Noah's clothes. They were a couple sizes too big, but she rolled up the sleeves and the cuffs, and she was alone most of the time, anyway, so who was there to deride what she looked like. At night she took to reading all the letters he'd written her from prison. He was a pretty good writer for a man with a third-grade education. He rarely wrote of prison. He told her mostly about books he was reading and memories he had of her and her mother. A lot of his words made her laugh out loud; a lot made her cry. She had a hard time sleeping. Sometimes, she had nightmares about terrible things happening to him. Sometimes, she woke so scared that she went immediately to her dun and headed for town and the telegraph office, but there was never any word.

Every few nights, she'd have dinner with Father Madsen at the mission. Rosita put on a good spread. Joan just wished she could have eaten more as a compliment to Rosita's cooking. Father Madsen always said he wasn't worried, that Noah would be fine, but Rosita told her in secret that the priest hardly slept and that he was given to moods and outbursts and had even been heard cursing aloud. This, Rosita said, was not the behavior of a man who is not worried. Rosita also said that there were certain Mexican saints who were especially good at protecting travelers. And so she prayed to them, prayed until her knees hurt. And then she gave Joan one of her bone-jarring bear hugs.

Joan also took to going to the mail station three times a week. But just as there was never anything for her at the telegraph station, neither was there anything for her with the mail.

Three weeks had gone by.

Noah found himself a place in Dryden.

The bank Tom Rattigan was president of was a Gothic Revival-style confection of pointed windows and gabled roofs. You half-expected to see plumed and helmeted Austrian guards come goose-stepping out the front door. It was the showplace of Dryden.

Noah never went inside. Instead he sat in a café across the street and watched a smart surrey pull up every morning and let Rattigan off for work. A liveried Negro drove the surrey. Rattigan hadn't changed much. The clothes, which were European-styled, the fashion of the moment, were expensive and peerless. Rattigan, as he'd always wanted to be, was New York in the middle of nowhere.

The easy thing for Noah to do would be to confront the man, but Rattigan would know the police chief well and Noah would end up in jail — and back in prison for violating parole.

He began following Rattigan — where Rattigan lived, went to church, the location and identity of the lodge he belonged to, where his daughter's horse was stabled, and where he took his wife to dine of an evening. Interesting, perhaps, but of no use whatsoever.

It became his habit to follow Rattigan home each night and tuck him in, as it were. Make sure that Rattigan was inside, enjoying his silk robe and cigar and brandy. Noah could then assume that Rattigan would be going no place else until morning.

But one night he decided to walk around to the back of the large manor house and sit on the pile of cut wood near the barn. He'd roll himself a cigarette and enjoy the sweet, cool night air. What a relief this was after Arizona.

Around eleven o'clock Rattigan, dressed in dark clothes, tiptoed out the back door of his estate house. And then into a shallow wooded area beyond which ran a narrow steam, gleaming in the light of the full moon. An elegant white gazebo bloomed like an exotic flower in the center of the clearing. And it was there that Rattigan met the woman.

She was slender, dark-haired, and from what Noah was able to see of her, quite lovely. Her clothes were of Rattigan's social class and she handled herself with real grace. There was no doubt she was in love and not simply lust. They held hands, they walked along the stream, they held each other and said soft things he could not hear. Lust wasn't practiced this way; lust was urgent, and rarely tender.

Five days after he saw her for the first time, Noah learned who she was. He was sitting in the city park with the Union war monuments and the bandstand when he saw the chief of police, a once-attractive man whose face and body had been lost to fat, strolling the boardwalk with a woman all the men stared at openly. You couldn't help yourself.

"You know who she is?" Noah asked the man sitting on the bench with him. A faded Union Army jacket with all the insignia torn off was the man's shirt. His

28

trousers were stained gray work pants. He was probably five years older than Noah.

"Sure. That's Chief Petty's wife. Caroline. She's a beauty, ain't she? Between you'n me, it's lasted a lot longer than most folks thought it would."

"Oh? Why's that?"

"Petty — Walter Petty — he was a young patrolman and one night he was on his way home and he seen their mansion on fire. She comes from money — and lots of it — that one does. So he rushes in and saves her mother and father. They was practically dead by the time he got to them. So he becomes this big hero and she starts going out with him, mostly because her folks liked him so much — he didn't have no money but he come from a respectable family, his old man is a clerk at this here shipping company — and he asks her to marry him after a year or so, and I guess her folks pushed her pretty hard and so she married him. Her folks built them this big house out on Rockland Street, right next to where Rattigan lives. He's the president of that bank over there and don't he think he's something, though. Like to tear his eyes out with my whittlin' knife. He foreclosed on my brother, the sonofabitch."

So finally Noah got the information he needed. And finally he knew how he was going to handle Tommy Rattigan.

TWO

Joan had never stood on a railroad platform at two a.m. before. She'd had no idea how lonely it could feel, watching the moon-gleaming tracks stretch empty in both directions, seeing the darkened and empty depot behind her.

The wagon from the undertaker was there, an Indian driver in a business suit sitting on the seat as they waited for the train, which was now more than an hour late.

"You know the first thing I'm going to ask God when I see Him in heaven?" Father Madsen said.

She knew he was trying to help. She owed him a response. "No, Father, what'll that be?"

"Why trains are never on time. I'll say, Lord, you created the entire universe and everything in it runs like clockwork — except for trains. Now why should that be?"

She smiled and touched the sleeve of his work shirt. "Thanks for being here with me, Father."

"I loved him, too, remember. He was like my brother."

Sky and desert stretched dark and unending. Even starlight seemed dimmer tonight. Day would never come again. No sunlight, no flowers, no children playing. Just this perpetual night, this depot platform, which seemed to be situated right on the edge of the infinite abyss.

This morning she'd ridden into town past the telegraph office. And this time Quirt had come hurrying out. He waved her down and handed up the telegram. But just as she was about to open it and read it, his hand clamped on her wrist and he said, "I sure am sorry, Joan. I sure am sorry."

The telegraph didn't actually say much. Just that her father's body was being shipped back on a train that would arrive late at night. There would be a full explanation following in a letter, which she could expect to receive within the next week. "No one is being held in the death of your father. Both witnesses put blame on your father himself. Upstanding people, these witnesses, and I don't have much choice except to believe them. I got your name and address from a letter you wrote him three years ago while he was in prison. I will explain everything in a letter that will follow within seven days. Yrs., Chief of Police Walter Petty."

She'd burned the telegram, as if destroying it would undo her father's death. She'd sat in the back of the mission church all afternoon. Father Madsen and his young assistant priest, Father Michaels, spent the day repairing one of the mission's crumbling adobe walls. The older priest was a fair-to-middling carpenter. When he was finished, he came in to the church to say some prayers, and there he found her.

For a long time she didn't say anything. Just sat there. In shock. Numb. Feeling unreal. He wasn't quite three months out of prison — all those years she'd waited for him — for something he hadn't even done, and now he was dead.

The priest didn't force her to talk. Knew better. She talked when she wanted to talk. She'd been this way even as a little girl.

Then she told him. She didn't cry, and that was sort of funny. She was given to tears quite frequently and for various reasons. Happiness made her cry just as often as sadness. But now she sat cold and dry.

"Rattigan had something to do with this," she said.

He took her hand. "Maybe not, Joan. The way Noah left here — anything could've happened."

"Rattigan," she said defiantly, almost childishly.

"I want you to stay here at the mission tonight. Rosita will fix us supper and then you can have one of the rooms and sleep for a while. Then we'll meet the train."

She didn't sleep, sat at a lonesome window and stared out at the purple-gold dusk and the blue-black night. And still didn't cry. Wanted to. But somehow couldn't. Her period started, too. The usual cramps. Her periods were usually difficult. But tonight she scarcely noticed. In the face of what had happened, her period seemed a trivial, silly thing to put any mind to.

Rosita came in and tried to start a conversation, but soon went away.

Then it was time to leave for the depot, and here they were now on the platform, watching the engine charge into view around the bend an eighth-mile away, all fierce steel and smoke and speed, the most awesome and splendid beast in the land.

The Indian on the undertaker's wagon drew the vehicle closer to the platform, then turned it around so that the back of the wagon bed faced the tracks. He'd obviously off-loaded his share of bodies. This was just one more. She had the moment most bereaved people had when they saw how businesslike the undertaking people were. To them, this was just one more body. But didn't they have any comprehension of who this person had been and what his life had meant and how his kin were suffering? She wanted to scream at the Indian's silence — he should be sobbing! — and professional indifference . . . and then her anger died as she realized how foolish it was.

Oil and steam and heat were the predominant smells the train brought with it. There were three passenger cars. On one of them two very smart-looking women, probably Eastern, looked out their window and watched with great, alert interest as Joan, Father Madsen, and the man from the undertaker's unloaded the black-painted pine coffin and set it carefully in the back of the wagon. A conductor climbed down from the train, meanwhile. Nobody got on or off. He watched the coffin business a few moments, checked his pocket watch, and then climbed back aboard his train.

The undertaker's parlor was on the far end of town. Joan wanted to ride in back — alone — with the coffin. She sat next to it, laying her face on its top, stroking the shape of the box again and again as if comforting the soul inside. There was the lonely sound of the single horse pulling the wagon, a screech owl somewhere distant, and an old Irish lullaby coming in soft snatches from Joan herself as the wagon wore on. Noah used to sing the same lullaby to her when she was a child.

And then it was over. The coffin taken inside the undertaker's parlor. The undertaker's wagon taking them back to the mission.

And Joan, at last, in bed in an isolated room, moonlight ghostly upon her frail form, weeping.

Father Madsen spent two hours in the church that night. Alone. Just a few of the votive candles — green and yellow and wine-red — pulsing light into the deep incense-sweet darkness.

He was not praying, simply thinking. Next to him was the Colt-Frontier Six-Shooter he'd used in the war. And taken to the dry creek bed with Noah a few weeks back.

I'm asking you to help me be a good liar, Lord. I'm afraid for Joan now and what she might do. I need to convince her that her father's death was an accident and that she should forget about it and go on with her life. Even though I'm pretty sure it wasn't. Even though I have to fight my own nature. I want to go there and take care of Rattigan myself. I know I've taken a vow of obedience and a vow of helping all your children, Father. But I don't know if I can ever forgive Tom Rattigan. I really don't know.

He sat there for a long time. Every so often he would pick up the Colt and hold it cold and hard in his big hand. The war had shown him to be an expert killer. He'd even done some sniping for a time before the war moved down the Mississippi. There was an easy way to deal with Rattigan. A final way . . .

But like Joan, he needed to forget — even if he could not forgive — and go on with his life. Noah had been foolish to go there, anyway, just as Joan had warned him.

Forget, yes; and go on with his priestly life . . .

Police Chief Walter Petty had one vanity; his uniform. He'd had three identical ones

37

made up for him. A colonel in the war had once said to him, "People respect authority when authority respects itself." The uniform was blue with smart gold buttons, and resembled a Union Army coat with blue black-striped trousers. The shoes were high-tops with buttons, and their gleam could blind you.

He was wondering why his wife, Caroline, didn't compliment him this morning as he sat across from her — and their two young daughters — at the breakfast table. She looked inexplicably tired again. Petty was a heavy sleeper. It took a war to wake him. He wished his wife was the same.

"Daddy, are you going to play baseball with us tonight?" Jenny said. She was six and resembled him. Cara was the lucky one. She was seven and resembled her mother.

"As long as you don't try and trip me again," he said.

Elva, the black maid, said, "More flapjacks for anybody?" from the kitchen door. Most police chiefs couldn't afford maids. But then most police chiefs didn't have a father-in-law who owned half the county.

"I guess not, Elva, thanks anyway," Caroline said, pushing dark flutters of hair from her face. There'd always been a slightly impish quality to her particular kind of good looks. But as she got older, the impish quality faded and a true classic beauty shaped her long, narrow face. Then: "Now, what's this about tripping Daddy?"

Both girls giggled.

"I tripped him," Jenny said, "but it was an accident."

"Are you willing to testify to that under oath?" he said.

Both girls giggled again. They loved baseball. They loved their daddy even more.

He found himself listening not to the girls, though, but to his wife. And not to her words but the sound of the words. There was a forced quality to her breakfast chatter these days — hell, to any conversation with her — the same strained quality he found in her tired face. He'd come home unexpectedly a few times during the day to have Elva tell him that Caroline was napping. Thirty-six-year-old Caroline Petty *napping?* What about all the clubs she belonged to, all the charity work she did, the library board, the school board? Caroline Petty didn't have *time* for napping. And yet it had become an essential part of her regimen.

And from these thoughts sprang, and quite logically, the next one: *We haven't made love in more than a month. We used to make love twice a week at least. A lot more than that before the girls came along. But now it's been a month.*

Walter Petty was professionally suspicious as a police officer because it was his job. The innocent-faced young man being questioned often proved to be guilty; the slightly ajar door in the back of a store was rarely an oversight but almost always a break-in; the suspect fire was nearly always arson.

He'd learned a long time ago not to be suspicious about women. He'd had a lady friend once and he'd been jealous as hell about her, and he'd ended up making a damned fool of himself over and over again. For every accusation he made, she came up with a simple and truthful explanation. Finally, she couldn't take his possessiveness anymore and found somebody else.

He'd known from the first that he wouldn't dare treat Caroline this way. For one thing, there was always the matter of status. You didn't question your social better. And make no mistake, though they were husband and wife — for better and worse and all that — Caroline was the superior of the two. And for another thing, his social better or not, he didn't want to drive her away. He was so much in love with her that sometimes his feelings overpowered him, almost suffocated him. He could never lose her. Never.

So: breakfast. A lovely sunny morning. Two lovely sunny children. And a wife who was just going through some "down" part of her life. She'd always been subject to melancholy — hell, her own father had warned him about that, the way a horseman will warn you about a tic or quirk of the animal you're buying — and that was probably what this was. Just another period of melancholy.

Then he was up and lurching toward the smart black Stetson he'd left on the hook next to the back door. "I forgot I'm supposed to be at the city council at 8:30!"

"I promise I won't trip you again, Daddy!" Jenny said.

He peeked back into the breakfast nook and said, "G'bye, everybody, I love you all."

The girls said good-bye, and so did Caroline. But that was another thing lately. She usually walked him to the back door in the mornings. His horse was stabled in back, so he went out that way. But lately she remained seated and just waved to him. A smile, yes, but he sensed the same strain he heard in her words. Forced.

Was something going on here?

But there it was, that old suspicion that had destroyed his very first love affair. He needed to take control of his feelings. He was being ridiculous. Caroline was tired. Having one of her fits of melancholy. He should appreciate that even though she was bone-weary herself, she tried hard to keep up appearances, good mother, good wife.

We haven't made love in more than a month.

No time to worry about anything but the city council meeting that he would definitely be late for.

No time — and thank God. His suspicious nature had already begun to sicken him. If Caroline couldn't be trusted, who could?

The gunsmith's name was J. R. Randisi. He worked out of a small, shantylike structure that led you to believe the inside would be equally unimpressive. But the interior was an immaculate presentation of his craft and wares. A glass case displayed the handguns he had for sale, while the

walls held four vertical glassed displays of
his rifles and shotguns. His worktable was
wide, clean, orderly. Randisi himself was a
solid man with a salted black beard and
smiling brown eyes.

He watched her as she looked down at
each handgun in the display case. Not
often did he get a customer so pretty. It
was sort of an event, the way a girl like this
could stir a middle-aged man. Wiping off
his hands on his apron, he set down the
Navy Colt he'd been working on and
walked over to her.

"Help you?"

"I need a gun."

"Got a couple of new ones in the back."

"A used one would be fine. I couldn't afford a new one."

"You used a handgun much?"

"Mostly a Winchester. My dad's. For
hunting."

He glanced at her hand. "Something not
too heavy. Not too hard to fire or take care
of."

"You have anything like that?"

"Oh, sure."

For the next fifteen minutes, he showed
her various weapons. They settled on a
Colt Double-Action .38.

"You take me down by the river and

43

show me how to use it?" she asked.

"I was just about to close up for lunch anyway. Sure."

She was much better than either of them had expected. He used tin cans. The first three series, she got two out of four. Then it was three out of four. She had good instincts. She seemed to have great purpose, too. Randisi wondered what the purpose might be. Though he lived in town and knew of her father Noah, he hadn't yet heard that Noah had returned home in a coffin early this morning. Most young women like this, they always giggled about what inept shots they were. No giggling here.

She paid him out of a jar she'd packed with money she'd obviously been saving for some time. He sold her a box of bullets, too. He shaved his profit down some — the way she had to turn that jar upside down to get every penny told him she didn't have much money — but didn't tell her. She didn't look like the kind who wanted any charity. It would embarrass her, maybe even make her mad.

As she left — damn, she was a looker — he went back to wondering why she wanted the gun and what she was going to do with it. . . .

Her next stop was the lawyer, C. W. Cantrell, who happened to be a lady lawyer. C.W. was at the county courthouse and wouldn't be back till tonight. Joan borrowed pen and paper.

Dear C.W.,

I want to thank you for all the help you gave my father. You were one of the few people who believed in his innocence. We never did pay you off in full. That's why — if I don't come back from a short trip I'm taking — I'd like to leave you everything in our cabin. While there's nothing fancy, you should be able to sell off everything for just about what we owe you.

In appreciation,
Joan Grieves

One more stop for Joan. As a young girl, she used to climb a tree near the mission and watch Father Madsen work. His muscular body — he invariably worked stripped to the waist — glistened with the sweat that glazed his Indianlike tan. His garden was his pride. She often thought that his garden was the woman his vocation had denied him. It needed to be loved and nurtured like a woman before it would yield its gifts. And there was no better lover than this man. Sometimes, when he would pluck a vegetable from the ground or a fruit from a tree, his face would grin like a boy's. Never were his patience and pride and love more expressive than in these moments. And she was patient, too, watching him for an hour, sometimes two. With her father dead now, the only person she felt close to was the priest.

She spent two hours in the tree today.

Sometimes, a breeze would come and she would lie back against a branch and close her eyes and remember the days — or was this all a fantasy she'd concocted to make herself feel better? — when both her parents were alive. And young. And healthy. And living. How they'd spoiled her — at least this was the way she'd chosen to remember it — and how they'd loved her. Then her mother was dead and her father was in prison and there was only Father Madsen. . . .

The undertaker came up on his horse and dismounted. He spoke earnestly to the priest, a stout man in a city suit far too hot for this day. They could be discussing only one thing: payment for the funeral. Father Madsen had already told her he would take care of it. She hoped he wouldn't hate her for slipping out of town before the funeral. There was only one reality now: Rattigan. Not even burying her father mattered. That was just a formality. She had enough money for the train trip and two nights' lodging and that was all. But that was all she needed.

She stayed a while longer, watching the priest work carefully with his hoe, not wanting to hurt, not wanting to injure, very crafty for a man of his size. *Please understand me, Father. Please understand that this is the only thing I can do. This man Rattigan destroyed my father and now he's destroyed me. I know you say that only the Lord should decide who should live and who should die, but I can't let Rattigan live any longer. Not and have my dignity or my sanity. Please understand me, Father. And forgive me and try to understand me at least a little bit. I love you, Father. I love you.*

In the late afternoon, the sun beginning to turn sky and desert and mountains radiantly bloody, she packed her war bag and went out to the horse and goat and dog, and gave them each a kiss on the head and then set off for town. The train wouldn't be here for another four hours. She would've taken the horse, but she wanted to leave it there so the lawyer C.W. could find it easily and sell it.

Not until she was halfway to town did she realize that she hadn't eaten anything since last night when Rosita had forced some food down her. But her grief and the heat had shrunk her stomach as well as her soul, and not even now did the thought of food appeal to her. Not even now.

In the afternoon, MacReady, one of Petty's patrolmen, leaned in the doorway of the chief's office and said, "I just took Red Carney home, Chief."

"Oh, shit," Petty said, looking up from his paperwork. "Drunk?"

"Damn near passed out. Was out at Stu Rumley's place, supposedly warning Stu about letting his horses wander into town the way he does. But Stu's got that still out there and —"

"Red just got drunk? Nothing else?"

"Nothing else. The poor bastard. He's such a damned nice guy."

"Thanks for telling me," Petty said.

He rolled himself a cigarette and finished up his cold coffee. Red Carney was a decent young man with a wife and kids. He had one problem: He was a drunkard. He could go dry three months or so, but that was about it. Then he'd get drunk and then Petty would suspend him for a couple of weeks. Everybody liked Red. He was a soft-spoken man who went to Mass every Sunday and was nice to everybody.

He was valuable to Petty for a specific reason. In a real sense, Petty owned him. The things Petty secretly made Carney do he wouldn't dare ask any of his other men to do. Carney had planted evidence on people; had followed people and spied on them when Petty demanded it. Carney hated it, of course. He was ashamed of the things he did. But what choice did he have? Not only could Petty fire Carney — he could also get him in legal trouble. One time Carney had done something pathetically stupid. He'd been drunk, of course. Any time Carney balked at doing Petty's bidding . . . all Petty had to do was bring up a certain incident. . . .

So now, Red Carney had fallen off the wagon again. He'd almost certainly made it two months dry this time. The poor bastard.

Father Madsen was in his study when Rosita knocked on his door. "The lawyer lady is here, Padre. She said it is much urgent."

The priest looked up from his magazine and took the pipe from his mouth. "Bring her in, Rosita."

Two minutes later, C. W. Cantrell, the most successful female lawyer in all the Territory, rushed in. C.W. of the massive bosom, of the pince-nez glasses, of the gray and somewhat mannish business suits, of middle-aged rectitude and unforgiving gaze. The odd thing was, despite her usually gruff pose, she had a quite beautiful face.

"This should explain why I'm here, Father," she said. She was somewhat breathless. "I just got back into town and found this on my desk. That child is going to get herself killed."

Madsen read Joan's note with growing anger. She was old enough to reason things through. Why would she do something this foolish? And then he realized that he was being unfair. In a very real sense, Tommy Rattigan had destroyed her life. Taken her father from her. Vengeance seemed the only answer.

"I need to get to the depot," he said, handing the note back.

The lawyer shook her head. "That was my first thought, Father. But it's too late. The train left half an hour ago." She took the note and slid it into the pocket of her jacket. "You'll have to go after her, Father. I'd go myself but she won't listen to me. You're the only one who can stop her."

He didn't get much sleep that night. He spent two hours going over everything with his young assistant pastor. What needed to be done, who needed to be seen. The young priest was nervous about being left in charge. A good thing he didn't know how nervous Madsen was about *leaving* him in charge.

Madsen packed two sets of clothes, neither clerical. He was going after her not as her priest but as her friend. He didn't want to embarrass or encumber his Church with anything he might be forced to say or do.

He took down his holster and six-shooter. He filled the holster belt with cartridges. Then he lay down and slept. He had dreams of her storming up to Rattigan and assassinating him the moment she saw him. That was the danger now. If he took the first train tomorrow, could he reach Dryden in time to stop her?

He said prayers. And then he fell into a light and troubled sleep.

THREE

"Well, Dryden may be a nice, safe town now," the talker said, "but it sure wasn't back in the days when the 'Paches were roamin' this part of the country, I'll tell you that much. That whole business district they got, that's where the first settlers built their houses. They had so many Indian attacks they had to build tunnels under their houses to hide in. One Indian attack after another. That's why the cavalry practically had to camp out there for years."

A talker. On train trips, Madsen had noted long ago, there were basically two types of people: talkers and listeners. Listeners endured; talkers talked.

This particular man was a drummer. Dry goods, he said. He even showed the priest his illustrated brochure. Shirts, cravats, trousers for the men; blouses, skirts, and chapeaus. Not hats — chapeaus. The man was skinny, angular, and all nervous energy. Mention a town or a famous person and he could give you a running history.

A short-run daytime train like this was filled with mothers and noisy kids, drummers, railroad personnel, and a wide variety of merchants and farmers. Short-runs never went far.

The two men got on in the middle of the hot morning. Madsen recognized them immediately. Karl and Leonard Schmitt. They recognized him, too. Priest and brothers exchanged scowls. They weren't much older than Joan but they'd already served a stretch in prison. They used to hang out in town and around the mission in particular. A few of the mission kids thought the would-be outlaws were pretty fancy. The brothers did look the part, right out of dime novels with their tight, dark clothes, low-brimmed dark hats, and tied-down Colts. They were the sort who had a smirk for anything that was decent and a fist for anybody who stood in their way.

Karl was the smart one and not completely unkind — Madsen had seen Karl fling himself in front of a wagon that was about to run over a little girl's foot. The girl was maybe seven, Mexican. He grabbed the girl, yanked her back in time.

He could've been badly injured himself. He could still hear (still shocking after all this time) what laughing Leonard had had to say: "Now, why'd you go and do something like that, brother. She ain't old enough to fuck."

One of the mission kids started hanging around them pretty regularly, enough so that he'd one day taken a swing at Madsen after Madsen told him to clean up a mess he'd made. Madsen punished the boy by keeping him in a week. Then he went after the Schmitt brothers and told them he didn't want them on mission property anymore. Leonard Schmitt made some dirty, smirking remark and Madsen grabbed him and flung him — literally flung him — against an adobe wall. He did this in full view of several young admirers of the brothers. Leonard wasn't hurt, but he was deeply humiliated. All that history was exchanged in the glances that passed among the three men on this train this particular morning.

The talker was still talking. "I had an uncle who knew this Comanche who had more than a hundred scalps. White scalps, of course. Can you imagine that, scalping a hundred men? Oh, and he was proud of it, too. Took my uncle right into his wigwam and showed him this whole stack of stacks. A whole *pile* of them? Can you believe it?"

Was it St. Francis who said that patience may be the greatest virtue of all?

If that was the case, Madsen was a holy man indeed. He endured the talker all the way to Dryden, where he and the Schmitt brothers — as well as at least half a dozen jumping-screaming-shouting kids — stepped off the train and onto the platform.

The Schmitt brothers gave him a parting scowl — they were so good at scowling they had to spend time in front of a mirror practicing it — and then disappeared into the crowds filling the streets of busy Dryden.

Tom Rattigan, Esquire (so he signed his name these days), came home at noon because when he'd left this morning his ten-year-old daughter Celia had once again refused to go to school.

His wife Molly met him at the door. "It's worse than usual, Tom. She's back to drawing the curtains again so she can be completely in the dark."

The mansion they lived in should have been resplendent with joy. The Rattigans were rich, popular, and generous. Wasn't

Molly (so sweet and pretty) always helping poor people with food and hand-me-down clothing and medicine? Wasn't Tom being talked about as a possible candidate in the gubernatorial election two years from now? Wasn't their oldest daughter Ellie already, at just twelve, a gifted viola player and an immensely skilled watercolorist? Didn't the Rattigans have looks, health, and the envy of all their friends (what was the point of being so wonderful if nobody *envied* you that wonderfulness)?

Yes (people would whisper), but they also had Celia, who proved that even people who seemed to have everything had their burdens, too.

Celia was ten. Her features were just as beautiful as her older sister's. Her skills with painting and music were just as formidable for her age. And she had inherited the Rattigan poise, as well.

But — there was the birthmark, a hideous, horrible birthmark — a large purple mass — that covered most of the left side of her face. Port-wine stain was the common name, hemangioma being the medical one.

The Rattigans had taken her as far as London to see if anything could be done about it. But nothing could.

56

Some days, Celia was fine. You wouldn't even know she *had* such a disfigurement. She went to school with the other children and had no trouble at all — from them or from herself.

But there were always mornings — such as *this* morning — when she awoke and felt monstrous. Truly — monstrous. As if she were the most hideous creature ever to escape a womb; as if every eye in the universe was upon her, and repelled. These were her dark-room days. Curtains drawn so tight that not a single sliver of light got into her room. She would not eat. Would not drink. Just lie on her bed, eyes wide open, staring. Sometimes, she stayed like this for four or five days at a time. Nothing could woo her from the back reaches of her cave. No word could comfort her.

"I'll go see her," Rattigan said.

Her room was on the second floor. It was a perfectly lovely room, and any girl would be perfectly lovely about having it. Unless the girl had a birthmark that covered most of the left side of her perfectly lovely face.

He knocked. "Honey."

The silence he expected.

"Honey, please, let me come in."

"Go away, Daddy. Just go away."

This was part of the ritual, too. The pleading.

"I won't stay long. I just want to make sure you're all right."

"I just need to be alone is all, Daddy. Now, please, just go away."

"I can't, honey, not until I make sure you're all right. It won't take but a minute, princess. I promise."

The silence he'd hoped for.

The first silence had been a go-away silence.

The second silence was I-won't-stop-you-if-you-come-in silence.

He turned the knob and let himself in. A sickroom. A dying-in room. Utter darkness thanks to the heavy drapes. All sight of Celia lost in the even-deeper gloom inside the confines of her canopy bed.

"Don't light the lantern, Daddy. I don't want you to see me. I don't want *any*body to see me."

And then the sobbing.

For a man of his anger, his cunning, his malice, his love and tenderness for his little girl shocked even him. He wanted to smite God Himself for inflicting such an affliction upon this innocent child. He knew how people treated her — the stares, the titters, the pointed fingers she had to endure. He'd heard her one night saying her prayers, begging God, *begging* Him to take away her stain. All his money, all his power, all his intelligence — and he couldn't protect the one person he loved more than any other.

"Please close the door, Daddy."

She didn't want even that much light in the room.

He closed the door. Came to her, pushing back the gauzy curtain hanging from the top of the canopy. He took her in his arms, and she cried more and he just held her, all the fury and clamor inside him useless.

She cried herself out, and then lay back in bed and took one of his massive red-haired hands and held it to her tear-warm face.

"Sometimes, I don't want to live, Daddy."

"Oh, please, honey, I've asked you not to say that. It scares me."

"I'll never have a husband. No boy would want me."

"Oh, sweetheart, that isn't true. *Lots* of boys will want you."

"They'll want your money. Or they'll feel sorry for me. But they won't *love* me."

"Who told you a ridiculous thing like that?"

"I read it in a book."

"What book?"

"About this rich girl who had a limp."

"It's a silly book, honey."

"No, it isn't. It made me cry."

He laughed. And then leaned down and kissed her warm cheek. "You don't need to cry any more than you already do. You'll run out of tears someday."

"Oh, Daddy." And he could tell she was smiling at him, and she sounded so young now, so young. "People don't run out of tears."

"Some people do. People who waste them all on silly books do."

"Oh, Daddy," she said again, and this time she sat up and slid her arms in her warm nightgown around him — her young-girl scent and her frail little arms. And this was the best sign of all, her sitting up like this, the first sign that this wouldn't be a siege of days holed up in here, but only this afternoon perhaps. With any luck she'd be down at dinner. She'd sit in the seat where the left side of her face was lost in the shadow of the candlelight, where nobody but the colored maid could see the stain.

"Sometimes when people look at me," she said into his shoulder, "I just want to run away. I feel so ashamed of myself."

He'd thought the worst of her grief was over for this particular round. But it wasn't. She'd never talked about being ashamed of herself before. Had never expressed it just that way, and it destroyed him, immobilized him for a time there, and she seemed to sense this because she held him all the tighter, and now it was Celia who was comforting him, saying, "You're so good to me, Daddy. You're the best daddy of all. You really are."

And all he could do was sit there, crushed by the random unfairness — this child shall have the hide of an alligator, this child shall be blind, this child shall die at four months of cholera — devastated by the incoherence of the universe. He despised his boyhood friend Peter Madsen at such moments, him and the certainty, even arrogance, of his God talk, God-this and God-that. Madsen had been a vicious killer in the war, and now he spent the rest of his life in remorse, or a ruse of remorse, pretending that his remorse could raise up the dead he'd slaughtered.

Finally, she lay back down and said, "I'm getting sleepy again, Daddy."

"I don't want to leave you, but work awaits me," he said, chucking Celia under the chin.

"That's all right, Daddy. I know you need to foreclose on some widows."

Their little joke. Their dear little joke. She'd seen a newspaper political cartoon of a cigar-chomping, bloated banker driving a widow and her flock of children off a farm — much the way Adam and Eve had been banished from the Garden of Eden. She'd shown it to her father, and since then it'd been their favorite private joke. Her parents were generous to people with less than themselves, and he'd told her (and her mother said that this was true) that several times he'd made mortgage payments himself just so he wouldn't have to turn anybody off their farms. She loved him all the more; what a fine daddy he was.

"I love you, sweetheart," he said, and kissed her the last time and stood up.

Molly was waiting anxiously for him at the bottom of the sweeping staircase. "Is she all right?"

"She's talking, anyway. That's always a good sign."

She touched his sleeve. And for a moment allowed her love for him to show in her almond-shaped, almond-colored eyes. But then last night came back to her — to them both, really — her waiting for him when he'd snuck in from his assignation with Caroline Petty. It wasn't his first such affair, and certainly wouldn't be his last. She just hoped that Caroline understood the rules Tom played by. He always came back to Molly and always would. They had a comfortable, sensible, ordered life together. And he could never leave Celia. The guilt would destroy him.

"Thank you," she said, and then turned away, her anger starting to work on her.

He took her arm. "About last night —"

"I should've complimented you," she said icily. "At least you're spending time with a much better grade of whore these days."

Then she pulled up the skirts of her fashionable organdy dress and hurried off to the kitchen.

FOUR

You could pretty much tell what kind of whorehouse it was by the smells. Or so said that sage of sages, Leonard Schmitt, one night when he stood blind drunk on the steps of a saloon and listened to a crib girl try to convince him to follow her back to the house she worked out of. There was a recession scorching the land; everybody was running from it. Crib girls were used to customers coming to them. But now they had to work the streets like common streetwalkers. Girls they just naturally felt superior to, even if the madams did charge ungodly amounts for crib rent.

"So how does this one smell, Leonard?" Karl said when they stepped into the vestibule of the whorehouse.

"What the hell's that supposed to mean?" said the burly, mannish-looking madam in the ill-fitting black silk dress. Black was great for hiding the numerous stains you could pick up in a place like this. "I run a clean house."

"And that's just how it smells, too." Leonard grinned, winking at his brother. "Clean."

"You better say that," said the surly-burly madam. "Otherwise, I'll kick your nuts up into your nose."

"And a Merry Christmas to you, too," Karl said. And winked back at his brother.

They were a pair, the Schmitts. Over from Ellsworth, Kansas, former cowhands, railroad men, casino bouncers, and bank robbers. The last had been their ticket to prison, where they had succeeded in getting two guards and one prisoner murdered without lifting a finger. They were crude, the Schmitts, but they knew how and when to spread the kind of rumor that could get the object of that rumor murdered. Now, they were back to robbing banks, with two disappointing quests so far in Idaho. Not much money at all, given the risks. Now they were here. Dryden was a booming town.

"What kind of gal you looking for?" the madam said.

"Somebody I can beat up." Leonard grinned.

"You lay a hand on one of my gals and I'll cut your cock off with a straight razor."

"And Merry Christmas to *you*, too." Karl giggled. They'd been three hours in town — which meant in a saloon — the robbery not being till tomorrow morning. For all his hayseed bullshit, Karl was actually pretty disciplined. He'd give them the rest of the afternoon and the early evening to drink up and whore up, and then he'd drag their asses back to the hotel. They'd sleep late, work off their hangovers with a brisk two-mile walk, take baths, eat a late breakfast, and then go buy themselves two horses for their flight from town. Then they'd hit the bank.

"Girls, get out here!" the madam snapped.

They'd been waiting in the other room. All Leonard cared about was breasts. They could be a sorry-ass specimen otherwise as long as they had big breasts. Karl was a romantic. He liked pretty faces. He'd even take them fat if they had pretty faces. He was the sophisticate of the two.

Leonard had a hard time choosing. Nearly every one of the girls had more than adequate breasts. Karl wasn't so lucky. If they weren't exactly ugly, they sure made a good pass at it.

"Pick one," the madam said. "Same way your brother did."

"I'm smarter'n my brother."

"Lissen to that sumbitch." Leonard laughed.

"You tellin' me you don't see one you like?" the madam said.

"I want a pretty-faced one." Karl nodded in the direction of the girls. "No offense, ladies."

"He's got a little dick, anyway." Leonard laughed again. "So you ain't missin' nothin', gals."

"Too bad Marla ain't feelin' good," one of the girls said.

"Who's Marla?" Karl said.

"Marla's on the mend," the madam said.

"From what?"

"Nosy bastard, ain't ya? She run up against a female physician who didn't know what the hell she was doin' is what's wrong with her." *Female physician* was slang for abortionist. Very few of them *did* know what they were doing.

"She pretty?" Karl said.

"She's damned beautiful is what she is, mister," one of the gals said.

"She's the one I want."

"Cost you three times."

"Pearl," one of the girls said, "Marla

probably shouldn't ought to —"

Pearl managed to attack her without moving. The girl shrank back as if a physical force had jumped on her. "You let me worry about what Marla probably shouldn't ought to, you hear me?"

The girl, abashed, nodded her simple sad prairie face and shrank back even farther.

"Cash on the barrelhead," Pearl said.

"Pay for me, Karl," Leonard said, grabbing his gal and heading up the stairs. "I'll pay ya back."

"Yeah," Karl said, "the way you always do. You prick."

Pearl had her hand out. After Karl paid her, she led him up the stairs and down to the end of a long hallway. There was no noise in a few of the cribs. Groans and gushes of pleasure mostly.

Pearl knocked quietly on the last door. "Marla?"

"Yeah, Pearl?"

"How you doin', hon?"

"Still kinda sick."

"Hon, I got one here willin' to pay you three times your usual. I'd split it with you fifty-fifty."

"Oh, Pearl, I couldn't stand to have no cock in me now."

Pearl said, "What if he went up your ass?"

Karl shook his head. "That's for nancy boys. No, thanks," he said. "Tell her I'll just come in an' have a drink with her and maybe I'll ask her to jack me off, but that'll be all."

"You hear that, Marla?"

"Oh, Pearl, I don't know. I just don't know. I'm just feelin' so sick is all."

"I'm just gonna send him in. He gives you any trouble, you just shout out and I'll come runnin'. You got me?"

"Oh, Pearl."

"He paid me already," Pearl laughed. "I never give nobody his money back and I sure don't want to start doin' it now."

"All right, Pearl. If you say so."

"He's kinda sweet sometimes, actually. Long as he ain't around that stupid brother of his."

"Hey," came a giggling voice from down the hall, "I heard that!" Good old Leonard, of course. "Hey, Karl, you want to see who can come the most times today?"

Oh, yes, it was Leonard; couldn't be nobody else *but* him. Talking, bragging like that.

"Go on in," Pearl said to Karl. "She's a real beauty. Just go in and see for yourself."

There was a café directly across from the bank. Joan sat at a table and stared at the bank's front door. She didn't know when he'd come out. She was going to sit here till he did. He needed to be real to her. In her mind, he was a monster. Not even human anymore. Less — and more — than human somehow.

There were people. Old, young, happy, sad, beautiful, ugly, drunk, sober. She didn't care. Didn't even see them except when they got in the way of her seeing the bank's front door. Then they irritated her. *Get out of the way, you stupid bastard. Get out of the way, you stupid bitch.* Words she rarely used in her life. Impatience she'd rarely felt. Only two people mattered now, her and Rattigan. She wouldn't even give him a warning. She'd just storm into his office and kill him. She could follow him away from the office and kill him. But she wanted him on the throne of his power. She wanted his underlings to see how vulnerable the great man was.

The long shadows came. Late afternoon always made her sad, the way rain did. Afternoon people were slower than morning people. You could see it in the horses and mules, too, how they were also slower. She drank more and more coffee. Got more and more agitated. Her period, too. What a time for her period. And more coffee. And no sight of him. *And so agitated. So agitated.*

And then — illusion? delusion? — she saw the impossible.

Father Madsen — but not dressed as Father Madsen — going into the front door of the bank.

"I'd like to see Mr. Rattigan, please," he said to the middle-aged woman at the small desk at the front of the long, narrow bank. On the right were four teller cages. On the left more desks where you went and talked to snappily dressed men in handlebar mustaches and spoke in the same reverent, hushed tones you used in the confessional. But here the god was money and not the Lord.

"I'll have to see if he's in," she said. "He leaves by the back way sometimes."

He nodded, stood there, looking around. It was an imposing place. After the war a lot of Western banks had taken to printing their own currency. They'd damned near destroyed the entire Western economy. But then both the federal and state governments started shutting them down and sending the worst of the bankers to prison. It had taken nearly two decades, but banks were again respectable. This one was especially so. A vast mural that took two walls to encompass illustrated key moments in the nation's history. The teller cages were mahogany. The floor tiling was tasteful and expensive. And everybody who worked here was just snooty enough to be impressive. Too snooty and you'd dislike them; just-so snooty and you'd think that maybe they were every bit as superior as they seemed to think.

The woman came back and said in a slightly superior way, "I'm sorry, he *did* slip out and go home for the day. Could you stop in tomorrow?"

"What time do you open?"

"Eight o'clock. Would you like to leave your name?"

"No, that's all right. I'll just stop back."

He stood on the street wondering where Joan was in all this hubbub. They didn't belong in a town like this, neither of them did. The mission was their home. They understood the desert and the small, primitive church and the peoples who had lived for generations in the shadow of the mountains. This was Babylon. Greed and lust and envy and perversion and murder. He felt sorry for those who lived here. Before the war he'd been like them. False gods. *Gold and pussy,* as the old saying went, *the only two things worth dying for.* But then he'd killed that woman and her child, and he'd learned through his torment and remorse how wrong he'd been. Mother and child, they were sacred. They were worth dying for. And he had defiled them. But he had learned, had grown, had come to understand what mattered. Joan mattered. Joan had to be saved. Joan was his daughter and sister and friend. If he had been a weaker man, he knew that she could also be his lover. He knew they'd both had moments when blood had leaned them in that direction. He thanked God he'd pulled back. Now he had to stop her, save her.

"How'd'ja meet her?"

"Oh, I never met her."

"You never *met* her'n you're in *love* with her?"

"It's kinda funny, isn't it?"

"I'll say. Fallin' in love with a pitcher. She sent it to ya when you was in prison, did she?"

"Nope. She didn't send it to me," Karl Schmitt said to Marla the whore. She was

73

pretty in an ordinary way, but not beautiful as Pearl had promised. She had a bottle of rotgut they passed back and forth. She said the female physician cut her all up during the abortion. She offered to let him *see* where she'd been all cut up. But he declined. He had this idealized notion of what a woman's pussy should look like. It should be clean and tidy and make you hungry for it. It shouldn't be all bloody and cut up.

They were at least one sheet to the wind, and would soon be two. Since he couldn't have sex with her and didn't really want just a hand job, he just sat on the bed with her, back to the headboard, sharing the bottle and rolling cigarettes, a few of which she took. And talking. Most of the time he had just Leonard to talk to, and Leonard wasn't exactly what you'd calling a sparkling conversationalist.

"So how you'd get her pitcher?"

"Found it in this cell."

"Cell? You was in prison?"

"Uh-huh."

"For what?"

"I killed six nuns and then ate a couple of babies."

She laughed and slapped him playfully on the arm. It was the most animated she'd been. "Oh, you."

"Bank robbery."

"You learn your lesson?"

He smiled. "Yeah. I learned to be a hell of a lot more careful the next time I hold up a bank."

She didn't laugh. "I got an older brother just like you. Twenty-four years old and been in prison twice. Just like Pa says, he's either gonna rot in a cell or be dead by thirty." Then: "So you found it in a cell?"

"The man who'd been there before me left it behind. Musta dropped out of his war bag or something. You sure wouldn't've left something like this behind on purpose."

"Why not?"

"Because she's so beautiful."

"The girl in the picture?"

"Yes, the girl in the picture."

"You got it on you?"

"I always got it on me."

"Then let me see it."

"I don't let nobody see it."

"Why not?"

"You know how Indians believe when a camera takes your pitcher that it takes your soul?"

"Uh-huh. But Indians are crazy."

"Not necessarily. That's how I think about this pitcher. I used to let other people see it, but you know what happened?"

"What?"

"It started to fade."

"It was getting old, maybe."

"Huh-uh. It was all those eyes on it. *They* were fading it. Because they stared at it so hard. Because she's so beautiful and they fell in love with it."

"With her or the pitcher?"

"Both."

"And you don't even know her name?"

"Not yet. But when I finish up with my business here in Dryden, that's what I'm gonna do."

"What?"

"What? I'm gonna find her, that's what. Find her and marry her and have three or four children by her and live on a nice farm and be happy and not give one little turd about anything else in this world except her and me and the kids."

"You don't even know her name and you're thinkin' like that already? What if she's married to the man who left her pitcher behind? Or what if you can't never find her? You gonna waste your whole life lookin'?"

"You sound like my brother now."

She laughed. "I sure don't want to

sound like Leonard." Then: "Oh, shit."

"What?"

"When I laughed. It stirred everything up all over again. Now it hurts."

"That's a hell of a thing. You can't laugh without it hurting."

She took a swig of whiskey. "How come you're in town?"

"Oh, just business."

"You're gonna rob a bank."

"Hey, don't say that so loud. Somebody might hear ya."

"I knew it. You're just like my brother. You never learn."

"I didn't say anything about robbing a bank. You did."

"You swear on your mama's grave you ain't here to rob a bank?"

"I won't swear on my mama's grave. But I'll swear on my papa's."

"How come your papa's?"

"Because," he said, "he hasn't got a grave. He's still alive and kickin'."

And then he wanted some sex. Sometimes, it happened that way. You were just sitting there talking, and then all of a sudden the damned thing took on a mind of its own.

"You just keep that bank business to yourself, you hear?"

"Oh, I hear, all right. You don't have to worry about me."

"I guess I wouldn't mind that hand job now."

"I still can't believe you and that Leonard are brothers."

He shrugged. "A lot of people can't."

"You ever kill anybody?"

"No."

She eyed him shrewdly. "I'll bet Leonard has."

"That wouldn't be any of your business."

"I'll bet he's killed more than one, too."

"C'mere," he said, and took her roughly to him. "I think I finally figured out a way to keep that yap of yours shut."

He kissed her almost angrily. She vaguely worried him, knowing about the bank the way she did. And he was angry with her for one more reason — for not being the girl in the picture. Everything he'd told her was true. After tomorrow, he'd have the money he'd need and he'd light out and find that girl in the picture. He had the name and whereabouts of the man who'd been in the cell before him. It was only a matter of time till he found the girl.

our father who art
hail mary full of
glory be to the father and the —

Joan lay in her shadowy little hotel room, beyond reading, beyond prayer, beyond redemption — or even distraction — of any kind. She was still greatly agitated. She had waited in the café till sundown, but had not had even a glimpse of him.

The coffee nerves were still with her, only adding to her anxiety. She could go to his house, but she'd probably just get arrested. Had to wait till morning. Then storm right in there. But how could she ever get through this night. The darkness stretched before her like infinity. She faced it without sleep or hope or any kind of real plan.

She was her gun. Literally. She imagined herself as a six-shooter pointed right at Rattigan.

She was also her father. Because as she killed Rattigan, she would scream out all the things he'd done to her father. Make him understand why he was dying at this particular time and in this particular way.

Or maybe she would turn the gun on herself.

She had never had such a thought until tonight. The coffee nerves. And her period.

They were combining to make her insane. Some kind of strange condition she'd never experienced before. Some total, overwhelming rage.

Could she hold out till morning? Maybe if she didn't kill herself tonight, she'd kill somebody else. It was that kind of fury within her.

Our Father who art

And Father Madsen in front of the bank. Big as life. What had he been doing there?

Her original thinking had been that she'd arrive in town early enough to find Rattigan and kill him. The priest wouldn't have had time to catch up to her if that had happened. But now she had to worry about him, too. Because he'd stop her. Oh, he'd stop her. Have her arrested if need be. No doubt about it.

Our Father who art

And for some reason, this time, her lips began to mouth the rest of the prayer. And the words — as they frequently did — began to comfort and solace her. The comfort and solace she needed to sleep. She needed to be sharp in the morning. Needed to be cunning and swift. Not groggy and logy.

She napped, and after a time woke up and saw the quarter moon in her window

— a fuzzy quarter moon, redolent of impending rain — and then she rolled over and sank into a deep sleep.

In the dream, she was at the prison gate. She was on a giant dun and held the reins of an equally large gray that was saddled and rested and ready for a long, hard ride. And then her father was there, a shambling, gray scarecrow-man. He still — inexplicably — wore his prison uniform. She could see that some unseen force was tugging him toward Dryden to the west. Where Rattigan lived. She wanted her father to get on the gray and ride with her. Ride to the mountains and the high desert, where he could start his life all over again. There was no point in pursuing Rattigan. None whatsoever. But her father startled her with his sudden strength and purpose. He hurled himself upon the gray and headed toward Dryden. No matter how fast she rode . . . she couldn't catch him . . . and this then became the dream. Riding hard after him but never being able to catch him . . . screaming his name . . . screaming for him to please for God's sake stop . . . but he was too determined. This was all he'd thought of when he was in prison. And so she was never able to catch up with him. He made it to Dryden and he found Rattigan. . . .

FIVE

He watched her as he had never watched her before. He watched her as one would watch a prisoner you might expect to make a quick and dangerous move. He watched her as if she were not a part of his life at all but an intruder, an unwelcome guest at the dinner table.

"Are you all right, Walter?"

"Fine, honey. Why?"

"You seem — distracted or something tonight."

He shrugged. "Tired is all. Long day. More trouble with Carney."

The children had finished their meals, and were in the living room. You couldn't talk about Carney around the girls.

She looked especially fetching tonight, did Caroline. He felt as if he were going to cry. He'd had little bursts of rage and grief all day. But this was the first time he'd simply wanted to cry. He had good instincts. She was hiding something from him, and he was afraid to know what it was. On the other hand, he had to know what it was. Had to.

"He was drunk again. In uniform."

"I wish I didn't feel so sorry for him, but I do. And his wife and children."

Dinner tonight had been roast beef and potatoes and squash. The maid was an excellent cook. The beef was tender. He pulled the last bits of it apart with his fork. Didn't need a knife. "Yes. This is the proof I need to fire him. I just can't let it slide this time."

Can't let it slide. Proof on Carney. Proof on you. The need for tears had subsided, replaced by a sick stomach. He was getting physically ill with this thing, the way he used to with his first lover when he'd imagine her lying by the river with anyone else.

He yawned. He had it planned out. "I'll sure sleep tonight."

"You sleep every night, dear."

Sleep so well you could sneak out without me knowing it. There was no other way it could be. She was busy all day with the children and her clubs. So, whatever was troubling her, whatever was tiring her out, had to be at night. While he slept.

"I'll sleep especially well tonight."

She leaned back in her chair. Usually, she'd make some comment about how much she enjoyed their moments alone at the end of the day. Not tonight. She stared off at some realm that was all her own. A man. He had berated himself lately for not trusting her. But now he was certain. He reached over to take her hand, pretend that everything was all right — he wanted her to believe that she was completely safe in her betrayal — but then he stopped himself. He couldn't bring himself to touch her. Icy hatred filled his heart. *Slut. Bitch. Cunt.*

He noticed then that his hand was trembling. His gun hand. He could feel the shape and heft of his Peacemaker in his hand. *He imagined killing her, round after round until his gun was empty, until her screaming had subsided.*

The maid was there next to him. "Would you like more coffee, Mr. Petty?"

"No, thanks."

"You, ma'am?"

"No, thanks. I thought I'd go in and play with the children."

If only she weren't so pretty. If only he didn't love her so much. If only she understood how much he loved her. If only she could un-

derstand that there was no man better suited to her anywhere in the world. If only she was more obedient like other wives. If only she weren't a conniving harlot at heart. I'll never give you the children. And I'll tell everyone in town what you've done to me and my children. Not even your parents will be able to defend you. I'll drive you out of town and you'll never see the kids again. Not ever. You'll die some diseased old whore, half blind and alone in some stinking filthy crib somewhere.

It was a litany of a kind — the litany of the spurned and cheated lover, and he knew the words all too well, almost in the way he knew prayers. Women — all women — every woman — would someday betray you as his mother had betrayed his father (he had seen his mother in the barn with her lover one afternoon, but had never said anything to anyone; six he'd been, and he'd seen the hairy blond sex of her where her dress was pulled up and her lover getting ready to put his cock in her — of course he'd never told anyone this because it would've destroyed his father).

She stood up. Just then one of the girls laughed. Such innocence. Hard to imagine such innocence had once resided in the treacherous nest this whore called a womb. He didn't want her to ever touch either of the girls. To ever speak a word to them. She was filth and they were innocence.

Amazing that he could sit there with the remnants of his coffee and his tailor-made cigarette and looking perfectly himself — master of his house, loyal husband, perfect father, chief of police, respected burgher. *And yet have these thoughts coil and uncoil and hiss and snap like snakes in a pit.*

Both girls were laughing now.

"Remember, day after tomorrow's Jenny's birthday," Caroline said. Ever the dutiful mother.

"I haven't forgotten a birthday yet."

Her harlot smile. "I couldn't ask for a better husband." And just for a moment — or had he imagined it? — a sorrow (was it too much to say *shame?*) in her dark eyes and her gentle voice.

He was afraid her shame, her sorrow would lead her to come kiss him. If he had to touch her flesh in any way, he would go insane. He had once arrested a man who had pounded his wife's skull into unimaginable bloody chunks with a two-pound hammer. Yes, that kind of frenzy would befall him, that kind of insanity would come over him, if she touched him in any way. *The touch of the whore.*

"Would you like to join us?" she said,

and the sorrow had not quite left her eyes or her voice. Perhaps she knew what lay ahead. That she would soon be banished from the house, and from the two people she loved beyond reasoning, her girls.

"No, thanks. I've got some paperwork to do in the study."

She nodded, and left for the light and frivolity of the parlor.

A few minutes later, he was in his second-floor study looking out at the backyard. So easy to slip out of the house, to use the darkness for your escape. And from there — where?

A shallow forest. A stream. The gazebo. And on the other side —

He smiled when he first had the thought. He had no doubt that his wife was a slut. But she still wouldn't have anything to do with a peacock like Tom Rattigan. How many times over the years had Petty heard her — and other ladies — make fun of his strutting ways and rampant unfaithfulness. Everybody respectable felt sorry for his poor wife, the way he cheated on her.

No, Tom Rattigan was out of the question, though Petty had to admit that it *would* be awfully convenient for the two of them — the gazebo being equidistant between the two large homes.

No, not Tom Rattigan . . . then who?

There was a small section of boarding-houses. Most of them had large RENTAL ROOMS signs nailed to the porch roof supports. Father Madsen checked out each one.

German, Swedish, Irish, Italian — each home had a different look, feel, and smell. None offensive. The people — widow women usually — who ran these places ran them clean and honest and good. In the early evening, music came from the parlors. Music rolls or live harmonicas or accordions or fiddles. A lot of the places housed railroad workers. Here and there you'd see a Confederate flag in the hall or the parlor, but mostly this had been Union country. All the women he asked questions of were curious. Husky, nice-looking older man like this asking for a young woman. Was he foolishly hunting down a woman too young for him? Was she his daughter? His niece? He never said. He left them with a lot of questions.

When he was done with the boarding-houses and sleeping rooms, he tried the hotels. The ones in the merchant district were too expensive for her. The ones near the railroad tracks were the only possibilities. When he walked inside and saw the type of man there — grizzled and sinister; or slick in cheap loud clothes — he hoped he wouldn't find her there. Anything could — and did — happen in places like these. He knew that she considered herself grown-up and capable of taking care of herself. But she'd spent most of her life in the shadow of the mission. Maybe she hadn't had much money, but she had been protected — she had had Rosita and himself as well as all the Mexicans and Indians who'd loved her since she was a little girl. All that protection was useless in places like these.

He didn't find her.

He ended up in a saloon having a beer. The language was filthy, vile. He had to smile to himself. These men would be stumbling all over themselves to apologize if they'd known he was a priest. That was always the way. But he couldn't feel *too* superior. While he took his priestly vows seriously, he'd never quite cured himself of the vile tongue — or vile mind. He'd lived too long in sin for sainthood.

He drifted back to the bank. He wasn't quite sure why. He imagined that Noah had stood in just this spot looking at the bank. Thinking about his life and how Tom Rattigan had changed it for him. Joan had probably stood here today, too.

He turned then — as if somebody had whispered in his ear telling him to — and looked at the empty window in the café behind him. The place was just closing up for the night. *What a good place to sit and drink coffee and watch the bank. Joan loves coffee, even though it ruins her nerves sometimes and she can't get a good night's sleep. Sitting in the window there. Watching the bank. Easy to imagine.*

He decided to go inside and ask.

A heavyset Mexican woman in a coarse white blouse and coarse blue skirt was cleaning off a table. There was a lot of noise in back. The help hurrying to close up.

"Were you here all day, ma'am?"

Her suspicion was evident in her narrowed eyes. "You are with the law in some way, *Señor?*"

"No. I'm looking for a young woman I know."

"I see." She smiled. "I hope this is a respectable relationship for a man of your age."

He laughed. He liked her candor. "I'm afraid for my age — and my calling — it is."

"Your calling?"

"I'm a priest."

"Yes, and I am the governor of the Territory."

"Believe it or not, I am."

She studied him. "It is not often you see a priest wearing a gun."

"I'm trying to prevent trouble. I don't plan to hurt anyone."

"Now there you sound like a priest."

"I'd like to describe this young woman to you."

He spoke two sentences and she said, "The nervous one. I asked her and she told me it was the coffee."

"She has a small scar on the right side of her face."

"On the jaw?"

"That's her. She fell against some barbed wire when she was younger."

"She is very sad, this young woman."

"That's why I want to help her. Before it's too late."

The woman thought a moment. "Ernesto, he spoke to her many times. She sat here a long, long time this afternoon. Ernesto is very romantic. He told me he was in love with her. But then he was in love with another one earlier in the day."

"Where do I find Ernesto?"

She gave him an address, described a street by the river.

The woman smiled. "Perhaps they are together, Ernesto and this young woman of yours. Ernesto, he is not much to look at, but many women find him very persuasive."

He nodded his thanks and left.

Rattigan spent an hour in Celia's room that night. She hadn't come down for dinner the way they'd hoped and expected. But at least her lamp burned brightly. She sat up in bed doing homework.

"You're going back to school tomorrow, I take it."

She nodded. "I have to go back someday. I may as well get it over with."

"You have a lot of good friends there."

"Not a lot. But a few."

"That's all you need. A few. I wish *I* had a few good friends."

"Oh, Daddy, don't be silly. All the people who come to our parties."

"They aren't really friends. Oh, your mother's friends. They're friends. But not mine. I'm the banker in town and they all want something from me. That's why they come to my parties. They think they're keeping me happy." Then he laughed. "I'm doing it again, aren't I?"

"Doing what, Daddy?" She was looking so cute and clean in her pigtails and fresh nightgown.

"I came up here to make *you* feel better. And here you are listening to me and making *me* feel better. Sometimes I can say things to you I don't even say to your —" And then he stopped himself. No, that wouldn't be appropriate to say to a girl about her mother.

"— That you don't even say to who, Daddy?"

"Oh, nothing." He took her hand and began stroking it. She'd always liked that, ever since she was a little girl. "And I shouldn't have said that about my friends. Some of them really do like me, I suppose. Enjoy my company and so forth. But they still want to keep me happy because they know they'll need me someday. Everybody needs his banker someday. It's like the parish priest — eventually, everybody in the parish ends up going to see him about one thing or another."

The moon was in the tall window now, so stark and winsome it looked like a painting. Not too long from now, Caroline would be in the gazebo, waiting for him. She was always there first, which lately had begun to make him nervous. Their relationship would have to end soon. Getting too dangerous. If it became public — if there was a scandal — he would be destroyed in this part of the Territory. Maybe even the entire Territory itself. And maybe elsewhere too. Who wants to do business with a man who made a cuckold out of another man?

It was so much easier getting into these things than getting out of them. Luckily, he'd chosen women who had as much at stake as he did. No scandals for them, either. He'd be glad when he was an old man, he sometimes thought. When the desire was a dry sac inside him and he no longer cared about the flesh. Then he'd know peace.

"Would you help me with this arithmetic problem, Daddy?"

"If you pay me."

"How much?"

"Two kisses."

"You want them both together, or one now and one later?"

"Hmm. That's a tough decision."

And then they both laughed and he took her in his arms and held her.

Something . . . strange about him to-

night. Almost . . . ominous somehow. She
sensed he was wearing a mask of some
sort. But why? Or was she just imagining
it?

They had just put the girls to bed. He
was in his study. At his desk. Working. A
handsome man limned by soft lamplight.

She knocked softly on the partly opened
door. "I guess I'll go to bed. I'm just all
done in."

She started toward him — good-night
kiss — but he stopped her. "I think I may
be coming down with a cold. No sense you
getting it, too."

"Oh."

Something . . . different.

*Oh, my God! Does he know about Tom
Rattigan?*

*No. Calm. Stay calm. Guilt is all it is. You
feel guilty and it's making you imagine all
sorts of things. He said it himself. He's coming
down with a cold. That's why he's acting so
funny tonight. Nothing sinister. Nothing ominous.*

*Maybe I shouldn't go tonight . . . but no.
How many nights had she said this to herself
and then gone anyway? She'd reached a terrible conclusion a few weeks ago. She was in
love with him. With Tom Rattigan. All her life
she'd wanted to be in love. Wildly, passionately*

in love. She respected her husband. A good man. And not just to her. To the kids. To the town. But she wasn't in love with him. There had never been a time when every other thought seemed to be of him. When her heart rate increased just at the mention of his name. When her entire body ached to have him inside her. When she dreamed dreams of running away with him . . . leaving everything else behind —

That was the most difficult thing she'd had to face these past few weeks. The knowledge that in order to spend their lives together — and she knew that he felt the same way she did — they would have to run away together like young lovers. Leave even their children behind. Even six weeks ago this would have been unthinkable. But in the last few weeks . . . the children would be better off with their father anyway. She knew she was an unfit mother — and she didn't even care. At least not to the extent that she'd give up Tom. Tom was her life. Her life forever. Nothing could change that now. She wouldn't let it.

"I'm sorry you're not feeling well, Walter."

"Oh, I'll be fine. Just a little head cold. You go on to bed now. You need your rest." He turned back to his paperwork.

How much easier all this would be if he

were a bad man. Not many women could claim husbands as nice as hers. And she was walking away from him.

Ernesto, it turned out, wasn't home. But he was down the street by the tracks in the neighborhood saloon.

The place was small, loud, dirty. Smoke. The smells of liquor and the outhouse on the other side of the back door. Sweat. Perfume. Half the men were Mexicans, the other half white drifters up from the rail yards. Some of them probably worked part-time at the yards. The girls probably enjoyed a good time, but they did not seem to be streetwalkers.

"I'm looking for a man named Ernesto Diaz."

"You the law?" said the wary Mexican saloonkeeper.

"Nope. Trying to find my daughter."

The man smiled. "That Ernesto. Always with the girls he's in trouble. I trust she's not pregnant."

"Not that I know of."

"And do you mean to start trouble?"

"No. No trouble. Just need to talk to him."

"Need I point out, *Señor*, that you are wearing a gun."

"No trouble. I promise."

The man pointed to a table near the back where an intense young Mexican man was talking to a very attractive young Mexican woman. "That would be Ernesto Diaz."

"Thank you."

"No trouble. You promised."

"No trouble."

Madsen made his way to the back. A big man like him a lot of people watched warily.

The girl noticed him before Diaz did. Diaz was too busy with talk of moonlight and romance. He had a weak, pretty face spoiled only slightly by the dishonesty of the eyes. The girl wasn't as pretty, but there was a sense of decency and amusement about her the priest liked instantly.

Madsen said, "I'm sorry to bother you. I wondered if I could talk to you, Mr. Diaz."

Diaz took suspicious note of Madsen. "You can't see that I'm busy here with my dear friend?" He'd said "dear friend" in a grand way that didn't befit his worn clothing or scruffy face. A poor-boy Lothario. Well, Madsen had been something like that, too, in his younger days.

"I'm trying to find my daughter. I asked at the café. They told me you spoke with her this afternoon." Saying she was his daughter was the most convenient way of getting through this conversation.

"I am too busy at the café to talk to anyone. I just work, *Señor*." This was obviously for the girl's benefit. He didn't want her to think he'd been flirting.

"You were very helpful to her. You told her where to find a room where she could sleep."

"I don't remember, I'm afraid."

"Somebody is trying to kill her. I have to find her."

The girl said, "Tell him, Ernesto. I do not care if you talk to this gringo girl. Tell him."

Ernesto said, "Truly, someone is trying to kill her?"

"Truly."

"I sensed much difficulty in her."

"Difficulty" wasn't the right word. But then Ernesto spoke English much better than Madsen spoke Mexican.

"I was trying to help her," Ernesto said.

The girl smiled. She knew her lover all too well. The gringo girl would have been pretty and Ernesto would have had many wild thoughts about this girl.

"It is true, Maria," Ernesto said, "helping her was all I was doing."

"Did you tell her about a place to stay?" Madsen said.

"Yes. By the river. There is an old house that Mrs. Sanchez runs."

"Mrs. Sanchez?" the girl said. "It is a pigsty. Why did you send her there?"

"Mrs. Sanchez gives me money for those I send to her. Those I meet in the café."

So much for altruism. And so much for flirting. Maybe this had been a strictly business proposition after all.

"You should have sent her somewhere else," the girl said.

Ernesto only shrugged.

"Would you give me the address of the Sanchez place?" Madsen asked.

Ernesto told him.

In the end, Karl Schmitt hadn't even gotten drunk. Marla had listened to his story and he'd listened to hers. Marla had gotten drunk. Marla had gotten *good* and drunk. There wasn't anything special about her story, really, though he supposed he felt sorry for her. He just couldn't imagine how a gal could just lie there in bed and let man after man fuck her. The fact was Karl didn't like men much. Being around other men was the worst part of prison. The way men smelled, talked, argued, fought, thought. They drove him crazy. Depressed him. Made him murderous. There was no refinement, no romance in men. Even when they had sex together — something he'd elected not to do, and the one man who'd approached him had gotten a badly broken nose for the trouble — they were just animals. All the time in prison he kept the picture of the girl with him, and nights he slept with it on his chest.

The picture was on his chest now. Leonard was sleeping off his drunk on the floor. Leonard had raised so much hell — firing his gun, breaking into one crib and throwing out the customer and jumping on the girl herself, telling Pearl that he strongly suspected she was a man — that a couple of black boys with sawed-off pistols showed up and threw the Schmitt boys out.

This was a robbery that was going to go right tomorrow. There was supposed to be at least $35,000 in that safe at all times, not like the penny-ante holdups they'd pulled right after getting out of Yuma. He was going to take his cut and he was going to say good-bye forever to his brother — it was one of those strange things where you could love a person (Leonard was, after all, his blood kin) and yet not like him the least little bit — and then head out and find the girl. And then his life would change. And that emptiness he'd always felt — the way he sometimes walked around on the verge of tears with no explanation at all for it, that damned sorrow that he'd never been able to express in prison because you showed any weakness and they'd be on you like wolves — and then his life would change forever. Forever. And he would live out his days with the girl in the picture, and to hell with all the people who'd told him he'd never find her and even if he did she wouldn't want him anyway . . . all the scoffers, all the doubters, all the sneerers . . . she would soon enough be his.

God, he wished Leonard would quit snoring. The wet sounds he made . . . he sounded just like a pig.

Karl lifted the picture then, and brought it to his lips and kissed her. He'd never given her a name. He knew that when he met her and she told him her name it would be musical, like out of a storybook. Not a common name, because there was nothing common about this girl.

Just before he drifted off to sleep, he started wondering about the bank. The way it had been told to him, the only guard was old and heavy. The way it had been told to him, there was always at least $35,000 in that vault. The way it had been told to him, the only reason the bank hadn't been held up before was because it was so far out of the way up in the northeast part of the Territory no robbers ever wanted to make the trip. The way it had been told to him.

He might have wished that his informant hadn't been somebody he'd known in Yuma. He might have wished that he'd been there to hear the man himself, rather than getting everything secondhand through Leonard. And he might have wished that Leonard had taken this whole thing more seriously and not gotten drunk so often the last couple weeks. You needed to be calm and cool. Otherwise you made a mistake. Their cousin Mike had gotten himself hanged because he'd accidentally shot and killed a bank guard. Simple little robbery, and then everything went wrong because Mike's gun accidentally discharged. Even the bank employees testified it didn't look as if Mike's gun had gone off on purpose. But they hanged him anyway.

God, he wished Leonard would quit his snoring.

God, he sounded like a pig.

SIX

Joan reached to the floor and grabbed her gun. People were starting to come and go in this rotting boardinghouse. A number of them passed by her door. She half-expected one of them to smash in and try and rape her.

She had been asleep, but now she was awake. Maybe she would be awake all night, the way they came tramping up and down the hall. Mostly men. A few women. Most boardinghouses wouldn't allow men and women both. Here it didn't matter. This was the end of the world, and the end of the world wasn't picky. About anything. Once or twice she could hear somebody puke. Then somebody cry. A woman. She wondered what she was crying about. Probably some man. That was usually why women cried.

A respite. Nobody moving in the hallway. Feeling she just might sneak back into sleep after all. It was like belly-crawling across enemy lines in a night battle. You had to get on the other side. And then sleep, blessed sleep, would close your eyes and slow your heart and . . .

She was almost there when the knock came. Instantly she reached down and grabbed her gun.

"Miss, there is somebody here to see you."

Was she dreaming? Who would be here to see her? Who knew she was here? She was still partly asleep.

"You mus' come down. I don' allow men and women up here together."

I noticed that, Joan thought, thinking of the men and women in the hall.

She was starting to come awake. A visitor — but who — And then: of course. Father Madsen. He'd managed to find her. Should have figured he would.

The bedclothes reeked. Probably hadn't been changed for months. She'd been so tired when she got here . . .

Had to think this through. Father Madsen wouldn't let her go through with it. That was why he was here, of course. To stop her. They would have a nice, sensible talk and then he would convince her to do the nice, sensible thing. Which meant going back to Arizona.

105

And forgetting all about Rattigan, who would go on with his fine shiny life and not care at all about the things he'd done to other people. That was what made her doubt God sometimes. The basic unfairness of life. He'd had her father sent to prison. And then he'd had her father killed and gotten away with it. And after she went back to Arizona, there'd be nobody to make him accountable for what he'd done. . . .

No, for once in her life, she wouldn't let the padre talk her into doing the nice, sensible thing.

"Tell him I'll be right down."

"I do not appreciate the late visitors, *Señorita*. This is a respectable place here."

And just then — who said that the dark forces of the cosmos didn't have a sense of humor? — a man a couple rooms down made a spectacular event of puking up everything except his toes.

She listened to the landlady lumber down the hall and then down the stairs.

She had no time to waste. Father Madsen would soon know what she was doing. She was glad she'd left most of her things in her bag. She grabbed it, stuffed the gun inside, and fled the room.

She had earlier noticed a back way out, and soon she was racing down the stairs.

After a few minutes, Madsen knew that he'd been had.

"Is there a back stairs?" he asked the skinny lady lost in her shabby night robe.

She nodded. Her eyes were luminous with some kind of sickness. Perhaps the cancer.

He thanked her, and then walked through the vestibule to the front porch. A man was passed out in a chair, snoring loudly, a pint bottle of whiskey next to him on the floor.

Madsen went alongside the house in the starry darkness. The sounds of night — dogs, trains, infants wailing.

He went around back and saw the back stairs she would have used. Then he went over to the alley and looked straight down it. There was enough moonlight to see her outline running north. She was too far away to catch.

He wondered what her plans were. He had to warn Rattigan first thing tomorrow.

At first, Walter Petty feared that he might actually fall asleep. Sentries fell asleep all the time guarding their posts.

Of course, he was guarding the most important post of all — his home. His wife, his children, his reputation. It would not do for the people of this town to know that their police chief was being betrayed by his wife. What would it say about him? It would say he was weak. So weak his wife had to find strength with another man. So weak that he hadn't learned about it until it had been going on for a while. So weak that he abided it.

Well, he wasn't *going* to abide it.

He was going to stop it before anybody else learned of it. And then he was going to give her her choice. Become the faithful wife again (though, Lord O Lord, she was going to pay in a million small, everyday ways for what she'd done to him and the children), or be publicly exposed for what she was. He knew that she would never choose the latter because she wouldn't want her children and her parents humiliated in this way.

He lay in the solitude of his marriage bed. She was pretending to sleep — just waiting for the right moment to leave — just as he was pretending to sleep. Just waiting for her to go and join her lover.

But what if I'm wrong? What if this is just my imagination? Well, wouldn't that be one hell of a nice surprise? All this for nothing. All this because I've got this damned jealousy thing in me. God, it would be so good if I was wrong.

At one point, tired of going over the punishments he planned to mete out to her — you could get tired even of revenge — he did have to fight sleep for a time.

Then (whispered): "Walt, are you asleep? Walt?"

He snored. Not loud, not theatrical. But a good, middle-range, deep-night snore.

And that startled him back to full wakefulness.

A long hesitation. Was she scared? Did she suspect he might be playacting? Did she wait this long every night she went to meet her lover?

She was child-light getting up from the bed. She'd probably had a lot of practice at this by now. Not a creak. Not a mattress sigh. Up and off the bed and gliding across the bedroom floor on her tippy-toes. A ballerina.

Pulling the door silently closed behind her.

His breath came in gasps now — rage — and his head was full of strange colors and noises, discordant, blinding, frightening when you added in the things his own mind was whispering to him. How he'd like to take one of the carving knifes from the kitchen and kill them both. *Slaughter* them both. He'd had a prisoner once who'd told him that he'd actually *enjoyed* the feeling of his wife's blood all over his hands and face and chest after he'd cut her up. And for days Petty couldn't stop quoting this man, aghast at his words. But now — O my Lord, look what he'd come to — he knew what the man had been talking about. He would enjoy Caroline's blood, too.

He tiptoed to the door. Listened.

She took something from the hall closet outside, then made her way down the stair-case.

He hurried to the bedroom closet. Pulled on his own clothes. His boots were downstairs. On his way down, he debated about the gun. It would be an awful temp-tation to use it if he took it along. This man's West was changing. Things didn't get settled with weapons at the rate they once had. A case like this would be settled in court — divorce and alienation of affec-tion. A scandal, for sure. But no one killed. Life just went on.

So he probably shouldn't take his gun. . . .

But of course, at the last minute, he did.

He took it and went out the door and went after her.

* * *

Rattigan wanted to make it quick to-night. In the beginning, trysts are always romantic as all hell. You don't mind the dew-covered gazebo seats. You don't mind the chill. You don't mind the discomfort of having sex on a wooden floor. You don't mind how tired you are in the morning. You don't even mind the risk you're taking, everything you're putting on the line just for a little strange pussy.

Ah, but doesn't that change over time (and not necessarily that long a time, either). The freshness begins to pall. The taste of her becomes familiar — not bad, just familiar. As familiar as your wife. And the feel of her. And the little tricks of her. And the laughter of her. And the conversation of her. My God — two, three months into it and she was so familiar it was like having an affair with your . . . wife. Indeed, you'd been so intensely wrapped up in this new one that you didn't spend much sexual time with your wife. So that after a few months . . . your wife was fresher to you than your tryst. And you found your-self drawn more to your wife than the one on the side. . . .

It was a strange old world.

Rattigan sat in the gazebo, smoking the

last of his stogie and watching as she slipped across the dewy clearing. She would come in a rush of sleep-smell and perfume-smell and sweet natural woman-smell; and a gush of words: *I love you O God I couldn't wait until tonight! Do you still love me, too, Tom? O please say it. You know how scared I am and how much I need to hear it. Oh please say it, Tom!*

He'd have to tell her soon. Like most things in his life — being a bank president meant that you had to be prepared for any contingency — he was prepared with just the right words for her. The process would take some time — four or five meetings — in the course of which she'd gradually come to realize that he was right. That their love would have to be set aside for the sake of their spouses and their children and their reputations. Theirs would be a love known only to them — a tragic love to be sure, but the only one they could continue with now that they'd come to the conclusion that they had to be selfless and adult about this whole thing. (Tom was a good one with tears when they helped his cause.)

And then she was in his arms.

"Oh, Tom, I love you so much! I've missed you so much!"

All sweet woman-smell as he flopped back the cowl of her cape and kissed her.

Yes, it would be a process that would take some time.

Petty could see her flickering through the trees, her dark cape and hood seeming to collect moonbeams and throw them back glowing, a firefly of a slender, lovely woman. And then she was lost in the knee-length grasses surrounding the gazebo, the dew radiant and sparkling beneath the vast sky, Caroline a figure out of a painting now, mysterious and eternal in the way of beautiful women. And there on the steps of the gazebo her man waited for her. No mistaking him, Tom Rattigan. And then they were embracing and in that moment Petty died a dozen times, each death compounding the pain of the previous one, all hope, all reason, all purpose dying with him.

And all he could do now was turn away. He couldn't watch anymore, not and be accountable for what he did.

They were lost to the shadows of the gazebo; Walter Petty was lost to the deeper shadows of his mind.

PART TWO

SEVEN

7:03 a.m.

The bank guard's name was Harold Dickens. He was sixty-three, carried the same pistol he'd carried in the war, and was liked by bank customers because his disposition was as sweet as his face. With his white hair, baby-blue eyes, and grand style of smiling, he was bound to be popular.

His duties began at seven a.m. sharp every weekday. He was the first in the bank via the back door. He then carried out the waste cans to the big incinerator in the back. A bank had an awful lot of wastepaper.

He'd timed this out once. It took him two and a half minutes to leave the bank building, walk to the incinerator, and then empty the cans and then walk back inside the bank. During this time, he kept an eye on the open back door. He usually checked it three or four times during the two and a half minutes, making sure that nobody snuck inside. Harold, needing the job, wanting the job, hadn't told anybody about the problems he'd been having with his eyes and hearing. He'd started missing things with his peripheral vision, and not since the war — standing too close to those damned cannons — had his hearing been all that good, anyway.

Joan didn't have any trouble sneaking in.

She'd been here three mornings in a row, watching him, deciding which was the exact best moment to run inside.

This was that moment.

Once inside, she knew exactly where to go. She'd also checked out the bank. Rattigan wouldn't have recognized her even if she'd literally bumped into him. Last time he'd seen her, she'd barely been in her teens.

She'd observed Rattigan in his natural habitat — ever the courtly, sophisticated banker (or so he imagined himself to be, she could see) — which was his office. He didn't like to leave his office unless it was necessary. He was always signing papers and giving dictation and standing at his side window looking out upon the town, his hands crossed behind his back, looking important.

She wore a blue gingham dress, her blond hair pulled back in a bun. If anyone looked at her, she blended in. Her six-shooter was hidden in the folds of her skirt.

She would never make it out of this bank alive. The thing was, she didn't care.

She hurried to his office, let herself in. He was a neat and orderly man, Rattigan. His desk held only a pen set and a small cedar box of cigars.

She heard Dickens coming back into the bank. She stepped quickly to the closet, let herself in, closed the door. This phase of the plan had gone very well. She was even running early. Rattigan wouldn't be here for another forty-five minutes yet.

She would let him get settled in for the day, and then she would step out of the closet and kill him. She had no plans for after that. She supposed Dickens would come in after her with his ancient gun from the war. She didn't really care. Rattigan was her only concern.

7:18 a.m.

Madsen was in place in the café across the street. The steaming coffee had cura-

119

tive powers. He inhaled the steam the way he'd inhale cigarette smoke. Sleep hadn't come till nearly dawn.

He looked around at the merchants and clerks getting ready for their town day. Every once in a while the idea of town intrigued him. Life was so different here from at the mission. But no, he thought, that's the old Madsen. The selfish Madsen. The people in and around the mission needed him. What with all the trouble they had with the U.S. Government — anybody with red or brown or yellow skin was automatically suspect in the eyes of the government — they needed a good friend to help them. The mother and the daughter he'd killed, they'd needed a friend, too. His sacrifice was a pittance compared to theirs.

He wondered where Joan was. Wondered if this was the day she'd try to kill Rattigan. Probably. She had to know he'd find her, stop her if at all possible.

He'd found a very early Mass in a Mexican church this morning. He'd offered his prayers exclusively for her. He didn't want to see her waste her life on Rattigan. Despite Madsen's occasional doubts about God's sense of mercy and justice, he believed that Rattigan would someday be forced to make spiritual restitution for all his crimes.

He sipped his coffee and stared out the window at the bank.

7:28 a.m.

Red Carney knew he was in real trouble this time. The drinking, of course, was what had done it. The damned stuff, he couldn't leave it alone. He'd gone nearly three months this time. Then he made the mistake of having a smoke in front of the saloon. He didn't even belong in a saloon, as his wife said. He was educated — ninth grade — he'd attended the police school twice in the past two years, and he was the assistant chief of police. The other men who lived on the street were workingmen. She didn't have anything against them, as she always said. But if Red could just stay sober, she pointed out, they'd soon be moving much closer to the part of town where the really influential people lived.

You couldn't ask for a more honest or reliable assistant chief of police . . . when he was sober. But when he was drinking . . . He'd listened to his wife shriek at him all night; now he would have to listen to Walt

Petty rag on him. Walt wouldn't shriek. He'd speak in a calm voice. But he'd make his point. And this time his point would be that no matter how much he liked Red, he'd have to fire him.

Carney wondered again why he couldn't leave the stuff alone. His life would be so much better. He *enjoyed* sobriety — for a while, anyway. Two, three weeks of sobriety, everybody encouraging him, especially his wife and Walt, it was great. He had his dignity, he had his purpose, he felt like a good and normal man. Why, he could go three months like that — once he'd gone *four* months — but then some little thing would set him off . . . some fit of temper, some disappointment, some tribulation would push him to the bottle. It would always start with beer, and then a few weeks down the line it would be whiskey. And it was always the same when his wife and Walt asked him about it. *I can control it this time. I really can. Just a couple of drinks in the evening and I'll be fine. You'll see. I'm on top of it this time. I really am.* And sometimes he would be on top of it for a while. He'd go another two months of a couple drinks a night and he'd be fine with it. But then, always —

Chief Petty's door was closed. He was in

there with the other assistant chief, Doherty. Carney had been told to be here at 7:00 a.m. The door opened up. Doherty, bald and freckled, came out and said, "You want to come in, Red? The chief wants to see you."

Carney tried to get a reading from the man's voice. Which way was the wind blowing inside that office? Doherty's voice was flat. No help at all. Carney stood up, nodded. His knees were shaking. He'd seen a man about to hang once, knees shaking so bad they had to help him onto the gallows. Carney wasn't that bad off, but he was afraid one of his knees might give out on him.

Petty was behind his desk, leaning back in his chair, his boots on the desk.

Carney started to sit down.

"Don't sit down, Red."

"What?"

"I said don't sit down." Then, to Doherty: "I'll talk to you later."

Doherty nodded, took a last look at Carney, and said, "I'll talk to you later, Chief."

The door closed.

Petty took his feet down and sat up straight. "You know what I want to do right now?"

"What?"

"Cry. And that's no bullshit. You're one of the best friends I've got. You're the best officer I've got. And now you've done it again."

Carney said, "I don't know what happens to me. I can't explain it. It's just when the urge comes —"

"Please, Red," was all Walt said. "Please don't make it any tougher for both of us than it needs to be. Just turn in your badge and gun. And your uniform within twenty-four hours. This time it's permanent, Red. I'm sorry. And I'm sorry for your wife and kids. But getting drunk — in your damned uniform yet — at an illegal still — you don't leave me any choice, Red. I'm sorry."

Carney dropped his head. Then turned and left the office.

That was the end of the conversation.

7:53 a.m.

Karl Schmitt had a bad feeling. He wasn't sure why, but things didn't *feel* right this morning. Leonard and Karl were eating breakfast in a café by the railroad tracks. The place was noisy with yard workers. The miners and the factory workers were long gone. Their day had started approximately an hour and a half ago.

Smacking his lips the way Leonard did . . . you'd think Karl would've gotten used to it after all these years. The way he should've gotten used to his brother's snoring. He felt guilty about it. He was smarter than Leonard. Leonard, the dumb fuck, couldn't help it.

"These flapjacks're tough," Leonard said.

"Maybe they've got jerky in them."

Leonard had duly noted his brother's sarcasm. "I don't have a right to say these flapjacks're tough? What jumped up and bit *you* on the ass this morning, brother?"

"You got drunk."

"So did you."

"No, I didn't."

"All the time you were in there with that Marla you didn't get drunk?"

"No."

"And you didn't get fucked?"

"No."

"Then you are one dumb sonofabitch. *I'm* s'posed to be the dumb one. But sounds more like *you* are."

"We agreed to quit drinking early."

"I'm fine."

Karl pointed with his fork to Leonard's

hand. "You call that fine?"

Leonard's hand was trembling. He'd been drinking long enough — whiskey wasn't all that hard to come by in prison — that he'd taken to having the shakes the mornings after. "So?"

"So. This don't feel good."

"*What* don't feel good?"

"The whole thing."

"We finally get a chance at *real* money and now you don't want to do it?"

"I didn't say I didn't want to do it."

"Then what *did* you say?"

Karl didn't like being questioned. He was, after all, the smart one. "I just said it didn't feel good."

Leonard talked around the mouthful of flapjack he was eating. The way he had to chew, those sonofabucks must've been tough. "You don't do it, I'll do it alone."

"Now there's a smart idea. Just how the hell would you do it alone?"

The big woman with the badly stained apron was back. "Anybody ever tell you two boys you look alike?"

Leonard laughed, crumbs of flapjacks falling out of his mouth as he did so. "They damn well should've. We're brothers."

"Well, I was kinda wonderin' about that."

Leonard nodded to the coffeepot she was holding. He always said things in such a way as to hurt people's feelings. He could just as easily have taken the polite way. But no, not Leonard Schmitt. The woman was at least two hundred pounds, so Leonard, in his meanest voice, said, "Little wisp of a thing like you. You must get tired of holdin' that coffeepot. You could pour some in our cups instead of standin' here jawin' with them stupid ideas of yours."

She wasn't angry. She was hurt.

Karl felt sorry for her, as he'd been feeling sorry for Leonard's victims all his life. "He didn't mean nothin' by that, ma'am."

"I can't help I'm so fat," the woman said, tears glinting in her blue eyes. "It was just the way I was born."

"I'm glad to know all that cake you eat don't have nothin' to do with it," Leonard said with a laugh.

"Shut up!" Karl said. "I'm sick of you and all your stupid talk. Now you sit there and you shut up, you hear me?"

And Leonard did just what his brother told him to do. Because there was another little secret about the Schmitt boys. Karl was smarter, not necessarily tougher. But when he got going, he was meaner, too.

Not petty, hurt-your-feelings mean the way Leonard was. He was crazy mean when he started fighting. Wouldn't give you a break. If he was slugging you, he'd slug you nearly to death. And likewise if he was kicking you. Or strangling you. There was one trouble — his moods. Sometimes he got so low he could barely function — and his moods came on without warning.

Everybody in the café was watching them. They sensed that if and when this Karl went off, you'd want to be in the next county. You sure wouldn't want to be anywhere around him.

"Thank you, ma'am, you done a fine job of servin' us this morning and I want you to know how much we appreciate it."

The woman nodded silently and withdrew.

"You like embarrassing me, don't you, brother?" Leonard said. He looked like a little boy who'd just been chastised by his parents.

"Once this job is over, I'm walkin' as far away from you as I can get."

"Feeling's mutual, believe me." Then: "So you're gonna go through with it?"

"I'm going through with it, all right, just so I can have enough money to get away from you. Way you treat people, you're gonna end up on the business end of a rope."

"And you're not?"

"I don't treat people the way you do."

Leonard sneered. Some of his fire was back. "That fella, you tore his eye out with your thumb that time? That a neighborly way of treatin' people, is it?"

"He tried to stab me. I didn't notice that poor woman who's been waitin' on us totin' a knife. Or maybe I missed something. I miss something, did I, Leonard?"

"I was just funnin' her. Damn, you're makin' a big thing out of nothin'."

Karl stood up. "Let's go."

"Where?"

"Somewhere where people aren't starin' at us. We're gonna rob a bank, remember?"

Now Leonard stood up. "You sure do push your luck, brother. But someday that luck's gonna run out. You wait and see. And you better hope I ain't there when it does, because I'm gonna remember how you been pushin' me around our whole lives."

Leonard was so much fun to be with. Karl hoped that after today he wouldn't see his brother for another sixty, seventy years.

8:01 a.m.

Thomas Rattigan, Esquire, was in place. Behind his desk. In his fancy Chicago-tailored suit. Ready to be friendly with robber baron and cowhand alike. If the celluloid collar pinched a bit, so be it. He looked damned good in such collars.

The bank doors had opened one minute ago.

There were those, of course, mostly the laboring types, who saw banking as a soft-hands sort of job. Not real work at all. But he would just once like to see these complainers deal with all the turmoil in the banking industry. There were a few states still issuing their own currency. There was the rise of the Greenback Party on the horizon. And the Silver Party that wanted the government bankers to restore the earlier ratio of silver to gold at sixteen to one. Without that ratio, the Silver folks warned, the economy would collapse, all paper money worthless.

And so on.

Soft-hand job, maybe; but certainly not softheaded.

The morning began. He had his coffee, his pipe — his employees had gently informed him that a pipe was ever so much friendlier to the air than a cigar, and did not lose a whit of masculinity — and his morning figures. Nothing remarkable in yesterday's report that he could see.

He was trying not to think of Caroline. Not to think of how she said she'd been thinking about everything and that they should run away — people did that all the time, she said. You were always reading about that in the newspapers and the magazines. And hearing about it. Two people just up and running away, leaving their spouses and their children. The loved ones were shocked and angry at first, she'd said, but later they always saw the wisdom of it. Saw that their marriage *had* been unhappy and that the spouse had actually done them a favor by running away.

California is where we should go. Have a completely fresh start. There are a lot of new towns in California. I'm sure they'll need bankers, the way their economy is booming. Not even the recession seems to be slowing them down. I've got a niece out there and she says that she's never seen so many wealthy people. She lives up north. We couldn't go to her because she'll have to take Walt's side in the whole thing — they like Walt very much — but we could go up somewhere on the Russian River, one of those towns there. The big thing is we'll be together. That's the only thing that really matters, anyway. That we'll be together.

The thing was, he never misled them, any of the women with whom he had affairs. He never so much as *hinted* that he would even consider leaving his wife and family. Even if he could leave Molly, how could he ever leave Celia? My God, she would be destroyed for life. He never even talked about his marriage. He knew that some men used the unhappy-marriage story as a means of seduction. *I'm just a poor lost soul stuck in a loveless marriage. I'm not at heart unfaithful. I take my wedding vows very seriously. But after a while when a man has a cold marriage bed . . . well, what can he do but seek comfort in the arms of another? In the arms of a very attractive, very* understanding *woman like you?* He never spoke many words. He was out for sex and fun and so were the married ladies he snuck off with. They rarely used the unhappy-marriage line either.

So how had it gone so damned wrong with Caroline Petty? She practically had them packed up and trundling off down to the depot and the next train headed for San Francisco.

The truth was, Caroline scared the hell out of him. Last night, he'd realized how unstable she was. God only knows what she would say — or do — next —

A sound. A *bump*. The kind of bump made when a knee inadvertently strikes a wall. Or an elbow nudges a door. Something like that.

A distinct sound. He glanced around his office. Empty. Sunlight on the glass of the bookcases. The scent of cherry furniture polish.

He glanced to his left. The closet. But what was in the closet that would make a noise like that? He stared at the closet door a moment. For the first time he saw that some of the mahogany along the very bottom was not quite as dark as the mahogany a few inches above. Less than a quarter inch of this lighter material, and it was gradational, it was dark and then light; it was more like it faded from being on the bottom. But still and all, it pissed him off. He wanted fine things; the finest. And he was willing to pay for them. And imperfections like this —

Well, at least the sound (whatever it had been) and the imperfect door had taken his mind off Caroline. Why spoil his day? Caroline would come around. She had as much to lose as he did. More, because the community would forever see her as a whore, as would anyone who knew the facts. Whereas he . . . easier for a man to recant and get on with his life. Molly would be outraged and humiliated, but in the end she would stand by him. And she would be in a position to keep him in miserable check the rest of his life. She could destroy him by divorcing him and charging adultery. And everybody would then know that he hadn't changed at all. And there would be a motion among the members of the bank board to get rid of him. A bank president needed a good reputation. . . .

He stared once again at the closet door. That sound *had* to have come from there. But what could it have been?

He decided to go have a look.

He got up from his desk and started walking across his office.

8:08 a.m.

Carney finally went to the saloon where the other law officers drank. At any given time you could run across a group of local boys and also a selection of marshals, sheriffs, and deputies traveling west to the Territorial capital to testify in a trial. Every lawman in the Territory knew about this saloon. Hart Jennings, the redheaded Irisher who ran the place, had been a lawman himself in his younger days, before his horse had crippled him in a fall. Hart had been chasing a killer, so he got a pretty good compensation for his accident and took that money and opened this bar. He was fifty-six and mean as snakes. Most of the time — as a favor to the rest of humanity — he stayed sober.

Carney had already visited two other saloons on his way here. He generally held his liquor well. But it was easy to see his anger and the way the liquor had fed it.

"Three whiskies," he said.

"Why don't I just give you the bottle?" Hart said.

"Because I didn't ask for the fucking bottle. I asked for three whiskies."

There were maybe a dozen men in here this time of morning. Half of them were retired; the other half were just common drunkards who also happened to be lawmen from various parts of the Territory. The latter group had never seen the Irisher behind the bar in action. They did now.

He brought up a double-barreled sawed-off shotgun and pointed it right at Carney's face. "You get your ass out of here, Carney, and come back when you can be civil."

The place was very quiet. The old-timers grinned and poked each other. They dearly loved to see Jennings put his sawed-off to some loudmouth's face, and Carney could be the loudest of the loudmouths at times.

"Go ahead and pull the fucking trigger, Hart. You'd be doing me a favor."

"Now what the hell's that 'sposed to mean, you dumb mick sonofabitch? And why ain't you in uniform?" He was sympathetic, but he didn't lower the sawed-off.

"He fired me."

"Who fired you?"

"Petty."

"For what?"

Carney shrugged. "Getting drunk out at the still."

Hart Jennings grinned. "You dumb bastard," he said, and laid his weapon down on the bar. He took a glass from beneath, filled it full of good whiskey, and then handed it to Carney. "Drink it."

Carney threw it back.

Jennings poured another one and handed it to him. "How dumb can you get?"

"Pretty damned dumb, I guess," Carney said.

A lot of men were still watching. Jennings waved them off. "You men mind your own business. Start drinkin' and talk or get your asses out of here, you hear me?" A polished host Hart Jennings was not. The men picked up their conversations again, knowing Jennings would throw them out if they didn't.

"So now what?" Jennings said to Carney.

"Now, I go home and tell the wife."

"I sure wouldn't want to be there for that one. You got a nice enough wife — and you know I mean that — but that little gal is gonna piss fire when she hears what you did."

Carney had looked miserable many times before — a man who drinks is a man who regrets — but he'd never looked *this* miserable. He held out his glass. Jennings filled it.

"I can't pay for all these drinks right now."

"Don't worry about it. Just don't tell nobody. Otherwise, I'll have every drunk within a hundred miles of here singin' me his sad song and askin' for free drinks."

"I just don't know what to do."

Jennings sighed. "Ask him for your job back."

Carney shook his head. "He wouldn't even talk to me now."

"Not today, Carney." He sighed,

scowled. "Think it through, son. Wait a few days. Get it over with your wife — she'll be pissed off at first, but then she'll be back with you in a few days. Go see Father Gomez and tell him you want to get right with God. And then find one of those little groups of men who're trying to quit the bottle. Hell, you're Petty's right-hand man. He'll take you back."

"I can't quit the bottle," Carney said, sounding horrified.

"You can if you want your job back," Jennings said. "And it don't have to be forever. Three, four months you can start nippin' again. You march into Petty's office with your wife, your priest, and a man from this group of teetotalers, not even some pussy like Petty can turn you down." He leaned forward. "What you got to do, in other words, is get back in his good graces, Carney. You can't threaten him. You can't wander around town pissin' and moanin'. *You got to get back in his good graces.* That's the only way, Carney, believe me."

And it was so brilliant, this plan, that it was almost as if his guardian angel had appeared to him and assured him that everything was going to be all right. He'd forgotten how wise and sensible Jennings could be.

And right there and right then, Carney started crying. And he didn't give a shit who saw him or heard him — he'd kill the first man who laughed at him — *he had to get back in Walter Petty's good graces!* Life could be so simple sometimes.

"How about another one of those drinks?" Carney said, and pushed his glass forward.

"My pleasure," Jennings said.

8:17 a.m.

Rattigan never did make it to the closet to find out what had made the noise. He was ten steps away when Mrs. Hodges, his assistant, stepped in and said that Mrs. Devane was here — a widower and the bank's second largest personal depositor — and he knew how she hated to be kept waiting. Mrs. Devane had no particular business — she'd just stopped by to get some cash for a short trip she was taking — but it would be unheard of for the president of the bank, one Thomas Rattigan, Esquire, not to step out of his office and greet her with all the insincere warmth (she was a dragon, this old lady) he could muster.

So he had gallantly gone forth and endured her compliments (how beautiful the bank looked after its recent redecoration) and insults (the teller in cage number three wasn't quite as nice — read: submissive — as she normally was), and general psychological overview (had he noticed that there seemed to be more and more riffraff in town these days, and when was Chief Petty going to do something about it?).

The vagaries of being bank president.

Joan, in the closet, heard most of this. Heard Mrs. Hodges tell him that Mrs. Devane was here. Heard Rattigan meet her on the cusp of his office and slavishly fawn over her. And then come back in and close his office door. When she heard him sit down — the chair made its own slight squeak — she opened the door and said, "Put your hands flat down on the desk."

"Who the hell are you?" he said, turning to watch her emerge from the darkness of the closet.

"Who the hell do you think I am?"

He looked at her gun and then at her face. "A lady bank robber. The newspaper people'll love this."

"Especially the part where I kill you."

He stared at her. Studied her. "You're

not here to rob me, are you? You want something else."

"I want you to suffer, that's what I want. The way he suffered."

He sighed. Sat back in his chair. "I fore-closed on somebody, is that it? Your father? Your husband? Your brother?"

She came over and carefully sat down across from him in the chair for customers. "You did a lot more than foreclose on him. You killed him."

His chair squeaked a bit as he leaned forward. "I sure wish you'd put that gun away, miss, so we could talk about this. I'm not the sort of man who goes around killing people."

"You don't kill them personally, no. You might get in trouble that way. But you blame them for things they didn't do and have them sent to prison — and then when they come at you with a gun, you have some sniper kill him for you."

The recognition wasn't instant, but it came pretty quick. He was studying her again, and then his eyes changed. He didn't seem absolutely sure of who she was, but he looked as if he had a pretty good guess.

"Joan? Joan Grieves? My Lord, is that you?"

"You killed him and now it's your turn."

"I can't believe it. The last time I saw you, you were a little girl. You were twelve or something like that."

She didn't say anything. Just sat there holding the gun on him.

"Joan, I don't expect you to remember, but you used to sit on my knee and I'd give you horsey rides. And I'd bring you little gifts every time I came to the house. Noah was my best friend."

She still didn't say anything. Just watched him. He was worth watching. Now that he'd gotten over the immediate shock of somebody stepping out of his closet with a gun — and now that he knew he was dealing with Joan — his mood changed. There was still tension in his face and hands — the faintest flicking tremor — but the grandiloquent actor in him had taken over. He was going to charm his way out of this. Or so he thought.

"Joan, I just can't believe it's you. You're such an attractive young woman. And the gun — doesn't it mean anything that I was your father's best friend? That I got him that job at the bank when nobody else would hire him? I know what he said about me, that I took the money and blamed him for it. But there were all kinds of people who knew the truth, including the judge and jury. They wouldn't convict a man on just my say-so. I had to show them how he'd taken the money and what he'd done for it."

He leaned even closer in his leather chair. "I even offered to let him pay the money back. Did he ever tell you that?"

"Why don't you just shut up? These are all lies."

"They're not lies, Joan. They aren't. Honest to God."

She saw what he was doing. How the trembling right hand was slowly working its way to the top drawer. There'd be a gun in there for just such emergencies as these.

He kept talking, and as he did so she got up and walked around the desk.

"If that darned bank examiner hadn't found that money was missing, I wouldn't even have turned Noah in. I would've just let him pay the money back quietly."

She stood at the drawer now. "Gun in there?"

"No. Just my tobacco. I need a cigar."

"You've got a box of them on your desk."

He swallowed hard. His fear was showing again. "Special cigars, Joan."

"Open it."

"I guess I don't want one."

"Open it. I want to see the cigars."

"This is foolishness, Joan."

"Open it."

He shook his head. He'd begun to sweat badly. She struck him hard enough along the jawline with the barrel of the gun to knock the chair back three or four inches. "Open it."

So he opened it — or started to — and she took her free hand and inserted his fingers between drawer and desk. And then she slammed it shut on him. A cracking sound; his knuckles.

The pain was such that he slumped forward, his head on his desk.

She went around and sat in her chair again and said, "Now, I want you to write out a confession saying that you took that money and blamed my father."

But that was as far as she got, because just then his office door burst open behind her.

She turned to see who was there, and got her answer faster than she expected or wanted. A man with a blue bandanna across his face. Holding a Colt on her and moving so fast that even before she could get up, he slammed the butt of his gun across the back of her skull and knocked her out clean cold.

EIGHT

8:26 a.m.

When the robbery started, there were nine people in the bank, six employees (including Tom Rattigan) and three customers. The Schmitt brothers came through the front door, turned slightly to the wall, pulled up their bandannas, and drew their guns. All this was done quickly before anybody saw.

Harold Dickens, the bank guard, was talking idly to a pretty teller named Irene Havers. Irene saw the red-masked Leonard before Dickens did. She made a funny, troubled noise in her throat and nodded to the front of the bank. Harold, no fool, understood instantly that there was something behind him worth looking at.

By the time he turned around to see what had spooked Irene so all-fired much, Leonard was standing two feet behind him. Leonard put his gun in Dickens's face.

145

From the front of the bank, in a calm, steady voice, Karl said, "You folks pretty much know how this works, so I don't have to give you a lot of talk. I want all the bank tellers to come around from behind there and lay facedown on the floor. Then I want the customers to do the same. If anybody screams or tries in any way to let anybody outside know what's going on, I'll shoot them. I'm not saying I'll kill them — I really don't want to kill anybody, I really don't — but do you really want to get shot in the leg or shoulder and have all that pain and discomfort and be laid up all that time? We're going to be working directly with the bank president. I'm going back to get him right now. The other man here'll be in charge. I hate to say it, but he's a lot meaner than I am. Between us, I don't think he'd mind killing some of you at all. Maybe all of you. Especially if you sic the law on us and we get held up here. That's something to keep in mind. Now, you tellers start filing out here."

The tellers had been told to do exactly what the robbers told them. Not worth losing your life, Rattigan had instructed them.

So they started filing out, obedient and quiet as schoolchildren filing into some school function.

"I guess I should've mentioned putting your hands up in the air," Karl said softly, almost cordially. "Just for the sake of appearances, I mean. That's how they always do it in those dime novels, ain't it? Their hands up in the air?"

The first thing Leonard did was take Harold Dickens's gun. He patted him down for any other weapons, too. Then he told the old man to lie down on the floor next to where the tellers were now lying. Harold Dickens had a pretty good frown, and he used it. He wanted Leonard to know that Dickens didn't like him at all. As if Leonard couldn't have figured that out all by his lonesome.

Leonard was in charge of the people on the floor. The bank floor that had been so big was suddenly small with all these bodies taking up the space.

Karl said, "Who locks up at night?"

"Donald does," said one of the two male tellers.

"Who's Donald?"

"I am," said the other male teller.

"Where do you keep your key?"

"Why do you want to know?"

"Because I have a gun is why."

"I could get in serious trouble, letting you know where the key is."

"Will somebody explain to Donald here that he's already in serious trouble?"

The other male teller said, "For God's sake, Donald, give him the key. You want to get us killed?"

But even this didn't hasten Donald's decision.

Leonard, who now stood alongside his brother, went over and gave the reluctant Donald a kick sharp enough to break a rib. Donald groaned. You could share his pain through the sounds he made. Nothing hurts much worse than a broken rib, especially if you're the kind who has to breathe.

"Oh, Lord, oh, Lord," Donald said.

The other male teller said, "The key is in his drawer. The second drawer. Don't kick him anymore. He started crying the first time we got stuck up. He shit his pants, too. Now he wants to show everybody he ain't scared."

"Shut up," Donald said miserably, around his pain.

"Just don't kick him anymore," the man said. "He's my brother."

Karl was afraid Leonard would say something stupid. *Hey, we're brothers, too, you know that?* But all Leonard did was coolly walk up to the door leading to the cages. He let himself in, went to the second drawer, and found the key. He brought it back up front, and then locked the front door and pulled the shade on the door window.

Karl went to work. He moved quickly along the edge of the bodies to the back of the place. Thomas Rattigan, Esquire, had his name on the door in gold.

The door was closed. But not for long.

Karl burst inside, gun ready.

8:32 a.m.

Madsen was the first one to see the shade pulled down on the bank door. The significance of this didn't register immediately. He sat with his cup of coffee, staring at the door.

Then: *Why would they be pulling the shade back down now? The sunlight wasn't at its blinding peak, they'd already opened for business, and why would they want to deter customers?*

Something was wrong and he knew what: Joan had managed to get in to see Rattigan before he did. She was holding him at gunpoint and had forced one of the employees to pull the shade down.

Madsen had walked around the bank

149

very early and seen a back entrance. No doubt that was how Joan had gotten inside.

He stood up, left money for his breakfast, hurried out the door.

Maybe the sun hadn't reached its zenith yet, but it was doing a passable job of pretending so. He felt lacquered by the heat, his pores clogged with it.

The west side of the bank sat on an alley of red dust. He took this, and went to the rear of the bank. Several horses were hitched there. A buggy sat empty. He went to the back door and tried the knob. Locked.

She was a smart girl. She'd thought of everything.

He put his ear to the door and listened. A strange silence given the fact that people should be talking and moving about.

A farm couple came down the alley and saw him with his ear to the back door. They looked as if they'd come upon a crime. He waved them away. They obviously wanted no trouble. They hurried on.

His next thought was of the roof. He went back down the alley so he could see as much of the top of the building as possible. He quickly saw that there was nothing for him up there.

He walked around to the front again. He tried the door carefully, quietly. Locked.

His instinct was to call out, rattle doors and windows and try and stop her. But that might only panic her. That might only bring about what he was trying to prevent. He could imagine her state of mind. It scared him.

8:36 a.m.

Between the liquor and the heat, Carney was greasy with sweat. His gait was slightly off.

He passed a number of people who spoke to him, but he didn't respond in any way. In his mind, everybody knew about his inglorious firing and they were greeting him out of pity or out of scorn. If he listened carefully to their greetings, he'd probably hear sarcasm. *There goes poor drunk Carney.*

The walk was helping. The liquor had been making him dizzy. Now clarity was returning, a clarity that told him he may as well go home and get it over with the wife. He'd send Ruth, who wasn't four and not in school yet, down to spend the morning at the Reynolds' house (Belle Reynolds

151

was also four), and then he'd sit down on the horsehair couch with the wife and tell her everything that had happened, with an emphasis on how it was all just a joke, him drinking it up out at the still — a joke Walt had taken the wrong way, darn him, anyway.

He had a moment of great peace. Of *course* the wife would believe him. She always had, or said she had, anyway. She had a sister with a bad-boy husband, and whenever the sister started complaining about the things he did, he'd just up and leave her and not come back till he'd had his fill of drinking and whoring. Is that what the wife wanted? Somebody who'd treat her like that? Hell, no, she didn't. No woman in her right mind ever would.

That was when he glanced to the right and noticed two things: the tall man gently trying the bank door and finding it locked; and the drawn shade behind the door window. *Why would the shade be drawn at this time of morning? And why would the door be locked?*

He might not have a badge at the moment, but he sure did remember the advice Jennings had given him. *You got to get back in his good graces, Carney.*

Carney broke stride and went over to the

bank to find out what the hell was going on.

8:43 a.m.

Police Chief Walter Petty was in his office when he heard the news. He was finishing up a report that the town council said it needed before they'd buy him any of the new firearms he'd seen on his last trip to the Territorial capital. Petty had their trust in all but the matter of weaponry. He had a tendency to view them as toys, and to tire of them as quickly as boys tired of *their* toys.

He was also doing his best to hold at bay any thoughts of last night. He had managed to sleep without letting on that he knew anything. So far as Caroline was concerned, he'd been in bed her entire trip to the gazebo and back.

He thought of forgiving her. No, he wanted to taunt her, which he planned to do with a series of blackmail notes. She wouldn't know who was sending them. She'd go insane with guilt and panic. He wanted to play his hand as long as he could. Wear her out.

As for Rattigan . . . he'd already killed

the man a dozen times in his mind. And one of these days he'd do it in reality. That he had no doubt of. Had to be the proper circumstances, though. So it would look like some enemy from the bank — some farmer he'd foreclosed on; some mining co-op he'd pulled his backing out on; some hotheaded rancher he wouldn't loan cattle-drive wage money to. A banker in Rattigan's position had an awful lot of enemies. And nobody would suspect the chief of police. Why would they? Not even Caroline knew that he knew about her and Tom.

He forced himself back to the report on why he needed half a dozen of the latest-model Winchester rifles. He had to be careful here. If he said that crime was rampant, it'd make him look bad. *So crime is rampant, Walter. Who the hell's fault is that?* On the other hand, if he made the town sound like a fantasy of peace and quiet, why would they give him any new rifles? *You say yourself that the town's never been any tamer than it is right now, Walt. Why would you be needing all these new rifles, then?*

Yes, indeed, he needed to be very, very careful. He had a real itch for these Winchesters. He couldn't wait to take one of them along when he went hunting with his favorite dog. (*Some nice images: a crisp autumn morning, him all bundled up and his setter trotting along next to him in the beautiful dew-covered fall fields, the gleam of ice on all the ponds, the crystal plume of his breath on the air, the wall of pines on the foothills beneath the ragged line of mountains, that peerless blue sky of fall . . . and at home a chastened woman who had learned that she was to be true to her husband the rest of her life . . . her poor Tom murdered by some lout he wouldn't loan any more money to . . . who could ask for a better day than that?*)

"*One reason our town has remained so law-abiding is that the police officers are generally better armed than the citizenry. This is one way — and we were taught this at the police school at the Territorial capital — that crime is deterred. An intelligent, sober police force armed with the latest rifles on weekends particularly — I don't need to remind you how many cowhands drift in here on Friday and Saturday nights — would certainly make any would-be lawbreaker think twice before he accosted one of our officers.*"

There. The weekend argument was a good one. Everybody in town had had some sort of trouble with drunken cowhands — everything from loud, vulgar lan-

155

guage to dangerously discharging firearms within the town limits. Drunken cowboys were apt to shoot at anything from lightning rods to store signs, not realizing in their inebriated state that this was how people accidentally got killed. Most of the cowhands were decent enough, just young and full of the wrong kind of energy, alcohol energy.

"I feel that given our overall performance as a police department, we deserve the most current equipment. And I have faith that you are sufficiently proud of our performance that you will comply with our request, even if it means that we have to add several hundred dollars to the existing budget. At our last meeting, we discussed the fact that the town would likely have a surplus very soon. I would like to request that part of that surplus be used to purchase the rifles I described in the opening of this letter."

There. Nicely put. No high-flow rhetorical flourishes (leave that to the mayor, who was apparently intending to go on the stage somewhere when he retired). And no bowing and scraping. That was one thing he'd never do. You could take all the other town functions — even put them all together — and none approached the police department in terms of importance. If you didn't have law and order — if the ordinary citizen couldn't safely walk the streets and the merchants couldn't conduct their business — what was the point of even having other town departments?

He heard the shout, and unflapped his holster and pulled out his Colt. A few times in the past madmen had charged into the department, waving a gun, threatening to kill the chief. Maybe this was another such incident. It would be ironic if the chief of police was found shot to death in his office at the very same desk where he'd just written a letter to the town council reminding them of what a safe town this was. The boys would be hooting over that one for years to come. He was not a beloved figure in this community and he knew it.

He sat with his weapon aimed dead-center at the open doorway.

Then he saw Briney, gasping and sweaty because of his extra thirty pounds, stumbling into the doorway, his gold-buttoned police uniform looking surprisingly tidy, trying to catch his breath so he could say what it took him several seconds to say —

"You better hurry, Chief. Somebody's holdin' up the bank and they already got hostages!"

NINE

"We don't want to hurt nobody," Karl Schmitt said. "We just want you to fill two big bags with the largest denominations of greenbacks you got." He looked at the woman who had slipped from the chair to the floor, unconscious. "I don't know who she was or why she was holdin' a gun on you, but I guess that shouldn't matter much to me. Now let's go to the vault and make this real easy."

"There isn't that much in there," Tom Rattigan said. As with Joan, he remained as cool as possible. They fed off fear, these people. It was their mother's milk. Nothing delighted them more than having power over you and nothing signified that power more than your fear. He recalled the last time the bank had been robbed — twice in all of Rattigan's tenure wasn't so bad — a

158

teller had actually shit his pants. And the worst thing was that they had been doe-colored suit pants. What a mess. What a humiliation. The man hadn't been the same since. It had always amazed Rattigan that the man had even come back to work here. Facing everybody who'd witnessed it six days a week couldn't be fun. And sure as hell nobody would ever forget it. Rattigan wondered how Donald Wayburn — that was the teller's name — was holding up during *this* robbery.

Rattigan would give them the money. And no tricks. Tricks — pulling out guns secreted away, trying to send signals for help to the outside, things of that nature — got you killed. *Keep quiet and do just what they tell you. Just remember that they're as scared as you are and that makes them very dangerous. They may not want to shoot you or plan to shoot you, but in their state the slightest thing may set them off.* He always said something like that the first day a person came to work here, after he'd explained, that is, that bank robberies were endemic in times of recession like this one. They always looked confused when he used the word "endemic." He was a stickler for literacy and vocabulary. He wanted to teach them new words (and frequently did) and he wanted them to work toward the distant goal of being literate — or literate as he saw it. Molly had pointed out many times that while he had taught himself a pretty decent vocabulary, he had yet to master proper English himself. She had been raised in far better circumstances and spoke the language without flaw.

"Here's how it'll work, Mr. Rattigan," Karl said through his bandanna. "You and I go get the two bags of money, and then you go out and lay on the floor with the rest of your people. You understand?"

Rattigan, his hands over his head, nodded.

"Now, we just walk out of your office nice and calm and walk to the vault. It's open, right?"

"Yes."

"Good."

"How about Joan?"

"We'll leave her right where she is. She'll be fine." Karl had already taken her gun and tucked it into his belt. "Now, let's go."

Karl stepped through the door and then waved to the banker to follow him.

Rattigan kept his hands above his head and walked sprightly. He didn't want anything to go wrong. You could always re-place money.

There was a good-sized crowd in front of the bank by the time Chief Petty got there. He didn't like to see this, and began barking for all those without business there to disperse. The two officers on the spot helped him push the crowd away. They dispersed, all right, but not far, taking to the boardwalks on the other side of the street, or standing beneath the overhangs of saloons and other businesses.

A tall man he didn't recognize came up to him. "I think I can tell you what's going on in there."

"Oh? And who might you be, mister?"

"My name's Madsen. I'm a priest. One of my parishioners is in there."

Petty glanced at the way the man was dressed. He looked like a hard-ass, especially with his gun tied to his leg. "You look like a gunny."

"I look different when I'm wearing my cassock."

"So where's the cassock?"

"I'm not here as a priest. I'm here as a friend. Last month her father was killed in that bank and she blames Tom Rattigan."

"Oh. This would be Noah Grieves?"

"Yes. The daughter's name is Joan."

Petty frowned. "Well, she's wrong if she thinks it was anything except justifiable homicide. He burst into Rattigan's office — her father, that is — and kept him there for over two hours. Every time I spoke to him through the door, he said he was going to kill Rattigan. I have a man named Carney. He was finally able to pick Grieves off through the window. Otherwise, Mr. Rattigan would be dead today."

Madsen believed him. "The trouble is, Joan believes — and I agree with her — that Rattigan killed her father a long time ago when he framed her father for embezzlement and had him sent to prison. Prison broke him. He never recovered, in his head, I mean. The first thing when he got out, all he could think of was getting even with Rattigan. He didn't care if he lived or died. He just wanted to square the debt. That's why he came here and did what he did."

"I'd put a lot more stock in your words if you were in your Roman collar, Madsen," Petty said. "If you really *have* a Roman collar, that is."

Not exactly what I want to see, Petty thought, turning away from Madsen and watching the figure running out of the alley toward him: Carney.

The closer the man got, the easier it was to smell the liquor on him. Carney had done just about what you'd expect Carney to do — go get drunk. Or start to, anyway. Carney didn't look completely pickled, but he was working on it.

He came up within three feet of the chief and said, "I got a look in the back door, Chief. There're two men in there with bandannas on. The tellers and the customers are all lying on the floor. Facedown. One of the robbers saw me in the door. They forgot to pull the shade in back. He was taking Tom Rattigan to the vault. Had a gun in his back."

"I didn't ask you to get involved, you know that, Carney."

"I know that, Chief. But I want to help."

Every once in a while, Carney was able to effect a boyishness, a near-innocence. God knows how a man with his history could work up such a charade. But at least it was a lot more appealing than his darker sides. And he *was* a good cop when he needed to be. He was smart, quick, and had some good ideas. And when you needed a sniper, he was maybe the best in the whole Territory.

This was the kind of job citizens of a law-abiding town wanted handled with safety and dispatch. No bloodbaths. No innocent civilians killed. Carney could be a vital part of insuring such an outcome. Petty didn't have another officer nearly as valuable. He wondered if Carney knew that. He hoped not.

"You get back to the station and get into your uniform."

"Yessir."

"And get the best rifle you can find there. Take my Winchester if you have to."

"Then I'm reinstated, sir?" He sounded boyish again, like a recruit.

Petty sighed. "Yeah, I guess you could say that. That thing we talked about this morning — you help me handle this and you have your job back."

"Yessir," Carney said. He looked as if he was going to cry out of sheer damned gratitude.

Carney offered him a brief salute. For once, it wasn't mocking. Carney was caught up in the moment. He obviously had a hard time keeping himself from grinning. The prick, Petty thought. He wins another one.

As Carney turned back to the far end of the business district, Madsen took his sleeve and said, "Did you see a young

164

woman in there? Early twenties. Very thin. Blond hair."

"No, sir, I didn't."

"You sure?"

"He said he didn't," Petty snapped. "He wouldn't have any reason to lie, would he? Now get back to the station, Carney."

"Yessir." He took off in a trot.

Madsen said, "I'm sure she's in there."

Petty said, "Maybe you're a priest and maybe you aren't. Right now, I don't give a damn either way. I just want you to clear the hell out of here just like the rest of the crowd. You want to watch, go up on the saloon porch or the hotel porch over there. Just stay the hell out of my way. There are citizens in danger — you never know which way these damned things will go — and I can't have you underfoot all the time. You understand me, Padre?" The last was offered sarcastically.

"I just hope you know what you're doing."

Petty smiled coldly. "Well, we'll know soon enough now, won't we? Because if I *don't* know what I'm doing, Padre, there's going to be one hell of a lot of dead people."

He watched the man walk away. He was a curiosity. There was a priestlike gentleness to him in some respects; yet in another way Petty sensed a cold rage in the man, too. He wasn't wearing that strapped-down gun just for effect. Petty had no doubt that the priest — if such he was — knew just how to use it.

And it was in that moment, turning away from Madsen, looking back at the bank, that the idea about Rattigan came to him. Here he'd lain awake half the night wondering how he was going to kill the man who had tainted Caroline. And now, miraculously, the solution had appeared before him.

He wasn't going to kill Tom Rattigan. He was going to let the bank robbers do it for him.

He was sure glad that Carney had forced his way back into uniform.

9:02 a.m.

Madsen walked down the alley to the rear of the bank. But Petty had two armed police officers standing sentry, complete with shotguns.

He decided to go back to the café, drink a cup of coffee, spend some time just seeing how events unraveled. There wasn't anything he could do at this point, anyway.

The café was crowded. There was a lone stool at the counter. He sat there sipping coffee and listening to various locals talk about how *they'd* handle the situation if they were the law.

"Petty makes a move on that bank," a farmer in a straw hat and acid-tainted chambray shirt said, "there's a good chance that them robbers'll kill everybody in there. They'll figure they don't have nothing to lose."

"Oh, hell, no, Byrum," said a skinny man in a worn business shirt, "they should give themselves up and nothin'll happen at all. They ain't shot anybody. I'd sure as hell go to Yuma for robbin' a bank than killin' a bunch of people."

"Tal's right," a waitress said. "If Petty doesn't go charging in there and riling those robbers up, everything should be fine. It's up to Petty, not the robbers."

That tended to be Madsen's opinion, too. While he didn't like Mr. Petty very much, he didn't envy the man the responsibility he had. One little wrong move and that whole bank could erupt in gunfire. It would take calm and steady nerves to make sure that everybody got out alive. He thought of poor Joan, her sad life. She'd come here for vengeance and was now being rewarded this way, by being a hostage, her fate in the hands of desperate bank robbers and a lawman with a great deal of preening pride. That was Petty's worst fault, as far as Madsen could see. The man thought well of himself and wanted others to think well of him, too. He wanted to give the impression of being in control. He wasn't about to let a couple of bank robbers make him look bad. That was a dangerous kind of pride.

9:26 a.m.

Headache. Confusion. Slowly gathering reality: She was lying on a polished hardwood floor looking at the sharp edge of a mahogany desk. Voices somewhere nearby. Couldn't make out what they were saying. But a definite urgency to them. Her fingers groped toward the wound on the side of her head. She expected to feel blood. But there was none. A goose egg was what she found. Good-sized one, too. Very sore to touch. Smells now: pipe smoke, cherry furniture polish, hot sunlight.

Tom Rattigan behind his desk. Trying to act calm in the face of her threat to kill him.

168

Putting on one of the performances Noah used to laugh so bitterly about. "Tom could outact anybody who was ever on stage. He was like that when we were six, seven years old." Then his eyes raising. Something going on behind her. Her first impression being that he was trying to just distract her so that he could swipe her gun away. But no, somebody actually there. A man in a blue bandanna rushing across the room, hitting her hard on the side of the head. And then blackness. And now —

Now, she pushed herself up from the floor. Now she felt her headache triple — quadruple — in intensity. It would be so easy and natural to just sink back to the floor and fall back down that deep dark protective well.

But no. Had to find out who the man in the bandanna was. Had to find out what was going on here. She wasn't through with Tom Rattigan. That was why she'd come to this town and she meant to finish her business. Whatever was going on in the bank now was no more than a mere interruption. She'd find Rattigan again — and get her gun back — and then she'd kill him. Just the same way he'd killed her father.

She fell against the desk. Couldn't really stand up straight and true. Had to grasp the desk edge as if it could keep her from drowning. The headache was thunderous.

And then she heard: "Look out the window! There's a whole crowd out there!"

She still didn't know who the voices belonged to or what they were so upset about.

She forced herself to stand up straight. Took a couple of deep breaths, the way Father Madsen had always taught her to when she needed to recover from a bad physical or mental experience. Then she walked, though none too confidently, to the doorway and looked out at the bank.

There had to be a dozen people lying facedown on the floor. At the front door, on either side of it, were two men. Slim, tall, saddle-tramp-looking men in flannel shirts and dusty dungarees. One wore a black, low-crowned hat and a blue bandanna — he was the man who'd knocked her out — while the other wore a white, low-crowned white hat and a red bandanna. They were very alike in size and movement.

They had pulled the shade back slightly so they could look out the window at the street. They obviously didn't like what they saw. Whatever was out there was what they were so frightened of.

Then she saw Rattigan. He sat in a chair next to the desk where the loan officer usually sat. There was a small woodcut on the desk that said LOAN OFFICER. He sat there, unaware of her as yet, watching the two men at the front door.

She was putting it together now. A robbery, of course. Robbers liked to strike quickly. In and out before a lawman spotted them or a posse could be got up. Apparently, from the way the red bandanna was talking, the townsfolk had been able to figure out that there was a robbery in progress here. Escape now was going to be damned hard.

Blue Bandanna saw her then. He said something quietly to his partner and then walked to the back, moving carefully around the bodies on the floor. Several of the people looked up at him, their faces tight with worry. A few of them looked as if they wanted to ask him something — understandably, they'd want reassurance that he wasn't going to hurt them — but his eyes were fixed on her. They seemed to rest on the exact top edge of his bandanna.

When he reached her he said, "You'll need to lay down on the floor, same as everybody else, miss."

"Is the law out there?"

He looked embarrassed, which she found endearing in a strange way. He'd been caught — and not at bank robbery but at not being very *good* at bank robbery. She knew just by his expression that the law had the bank surrounded. "I guess they are."

"So now what do you do? You look scared."

He seemed confused. "I'm the one who hit you on the head. Why would you give a damn about me?"

"Because I hate him, too."

"Who?"

"Rattigan. The bank president."

"I don't care about him one way or the other."

"I do. If you don't kill him, I will. That's what I was about to do when you came in and knocked me out."

"What'd he ever do to you?"

"Killed my dad."

From the front of the bank, Red Bandanna said, "You said you was gonna check the back door. Get your ass over there."

"He's right," Blue Bandanna said. "I got to cover that door. Check it out. And you need to get over there and lay down. You hear me?"

"I meant what I said. Either you kill him or I do."

"You don't have a gun."

"I'll get one."

Once again, she felt sort of sorry for him. He was young. He acted tough but he wasn't — mean but not tough. You went in and robbed a bank and that's all there was to it. Real, real easy. Except it wasn't. You had to make what military men called contingency plans. What if the law figured out you were holding up the bank and surrounded you, like now? What did you do then? Blue Bandanna obviously had no idea.

"C'mon now, get over there and lay down."

"Don't hurt anybody else," she said. "Just him."

Then she went and lay down.

9:56 a.m.

Madsen knelt at the communion rail. The altar of this Catholic church was like a cathedral compared to the crude wooden altar of his mission church. The Christ above the altar was polished silver and the altar itself marble. The church was small but finely wrought.

He had his rosary beads in his hands, the crucifix dangling, and his head down. There was the melancholy scent of incense and votive candles on the air.

When he looked up, he saw the ancient Mexican priest up on the altar replacing one of the holders with a new candle. He did this in three-quarters profile. When he faced Madsen, he looked like an Aztec icon, a fierce wisdom in his burnished eyes and wide, flat face. "You are troubled, my son?" the priest said. He wore a black cassock and a Roman collar. His hair was the color of purest snow.

"Yes, Father, I am." He hesitated. "I'm a priest, too."

"A priest? And yet you wear a gun?"

"I'm confused, Father. About the gun, I mean."

The priest did not soften the harshness of his voice. "There should be no confusion. If you are a priest then you should never carry a gun. The priests in my native country are killed every day on both sides in the war and yet they don't take up weapons. If you are a soldier of God, then you do not fight that way."

"I thought I might need it to protect someone I care about very much." He briefly explained the situation.

The old priest came down from the altar right to the communion rail. Madsen stood up, dropped his rosary in his pocket.

"I can see why you wouldn't wear your cassock and collar. But I still can't see why you would wear a gun. Are you planning on using it?"

"No."

"Then why not leave it with me while you're in town here?"

"What if I need it?"

"If you need it, then your calling to the priesthood is not a true one. A priest would not use a gun. Perhaps you are thrilled to be carrying a gun."

The words had more effect than Madsen wanted them to. There had been a few times in the past twenty-four hours when there had been a sinful pleasure in feeling the gun on his hip. *The old days. The hell-raising days. The women-and-whiskey days. And then the war years. The big, handsome man who was good with his gun. Not a legend by any means. But good with it. Enough so that people walked wide of him for the most part. His pride. His vanity. It was as if this Aztec-like priest had been able to peer into his mind, see both his past and his present, and see the truth of Madsen's heart. Yes, he'd felt he needed the gun to protect Joan. But there had also been an undeniable thrill in wearing the rig again. Wearing the rig and having people watch him as he strode down the street.*

"The gun will be here for you when you return back home," the old priest said. "You should do it now before you change your mind."

"You must be some kind of mind reader, Father. That's just what I was thinking. I'd probably better hand it over now while you've got me in the right mood."

"Oh, yes," the priest said, "reading minds is my specialty. For many centuries the women in my former land have known how to do such things. Some of the men can do it, too. But not nearly so well as the women." For the first time, the old priest smiled. "Men do not like to hear it, but I am afraid the women are our superior in most things that matter."

"I figured that out for myself, Father," Madsen said, unstrapping his gun belt and handing it to the priest, "even before I was ordained."

10:03 a.m.

Petty's men had cleared the street. Six people stood in front of the bank in the baking, dusty street. All of them Petty's men. Even the mayor and the town council had been consigned to the boardwalk.

Petty took his rifle and approached the bank alone. He called out, "I want to know the names of everybody you've got in there."

There was no response.

"There won't be any discussion of any kind until you identify everybody in there. You're holding hostages but so are we — you're *our* hostages. I don't know what kind of deal you men are interested in making, but we have to start with the names. Do you understand that?"

While he waited for them to shout back to him, he glanced around the street wondering where Carney was. Even a good marksman like Carney would have a difficult time figuring out how to get a shot into the bank. Both front and back doors had shades on the glass. There was no front window. That meant only the side window was available to them. And the problem with that was that it was more decoration than anything, a four-foot-deep, two-foot-wide rectangle in the red brick. The target would have to be standing within that frame before you could even think of shooting at him. And how likely was it that he would be standing there?

The front door of the bank opened perhaps two inches. "We want our two horses out back. We're taking the money with us. And we're also taking one hostage." All he could see of the man was dark hair and a blue bandanna.

"You heard what I said," Petty called back. "I need to know who is in there before we talk any kind of deal."

"What difference does it make?"

"None to you. But if you had a loved one in there — a mother or father or sister or brother or husband — you'd sure want to know, wouldn't you? Now I want a list of every man and woman in there. And I want it right now. Or, mister, we don't have one damned thing to talk about."

The bank door closed.

This time when Petty turned around, there were more people lining the boardwalks and the porches of the hotels and saloons. Common, everyday folks. Scared now. The same way they got scared at mine cave-ins and fires and drownings. Afraid that one of their own might have been killed or be in danger. You could see the prayers on the women's mouths and the granite fear in the eyes of their men.

But the men couldn't whisper prayers or show their terror. They'd been taught not to at such moments.

Petty was their man. A lot of them didn't like him, but just about everybody believed he was competent and judicious as a police chief. They felt a little better about him being in charge. He'd know what to do. He wasn't a hothead and he wasn't a showboat and he knew how to defuse a moment, take it down instead of up to chaos and bloodshed.

He understood — knew — all these things as he stood there in the hot street, the crowd more scared than angry now, the anger something that would come a little later as frustration grew. No way these boys were simply going to lay down their guns and walk out of there with their hands up. They had hostages and they were going to press for every advantage they could get. He'd do the same thing in their circumstances. But the longer they played the poker game, the angrier the crowd would get. And the angrier the crowd got, the more dangerous the game became. Because somebody was apt to do something foolish. It might be one of the robbers, it might be one of the crowd, it might even be one of his own men. It was going to be one tricky sonofabitch today. He needed to accomplish two things. He needed to get every innocent citizen out of that bank alive. And he needed to get Tom Rattigan killed.

The bank door opened. Blue Bandanna said, "I'm gonna call these names out one at a time."

"Not good enough."

"What the hell you mean?"

"I want you to bring every one of them to the door one at a time so we can see they're all right. You can keep the door closed. But keep the shade up so we can get a good look at them."

"That isn't what you said."

"That's what I'm saying now. And that's all that matters." You had to let them know that you could play poker just as well as they could.

"Well, that ain't gonna happen."

"Well, then we're not going to talk about how you might get out of here with those bags of money."

The door slammed shut so hard, Petty was half-surprised the pane of glass didn't fall out.

He looked west and saw Madsen coming down the street. The closer he got, the more Petty realized that something was different about the man now. Then he recognized the difference. Madsen wasn't wearing a gun now.

Madsen came up. "You find out anything about Joan?"

"I told them I wanted to see everybody who's in there one person at a time in the front door. Make sure nobody's been hurt yet. If she's in there, you'll see her soon enough."

"What if they won't go along?"

Petty smiled coldly. "It might seem that they've got the upper hand. They've got the hostages. But we've got one thing on our side: For the time being we can refuse to even hear their demands until they show us everybody in there is alive and well."

And that was just when the door opened a few more inches and Blue Bandanna said, "We're gonna put 'em in the door here one at a time. Then we want to talk about getting out of this hick town."

"No point in insulting our town," Petty said calmly. "It's a nice place to live — or was until you got here anyway. Now let's see those hostages you've got."

The door closed again. There was a two-three minutes time when absolutely nothing happened. Mostly silence except for the horses in the livery and the distant jangle and commotion of the stagecoach as it left town. Passengers and the mail had to get through no matter what.

The shade went up on the door. You could hear the robbers snapping at people to get on their feet. One at a time the hostages showed themselves in the door glass.

It reminded Petty of a grade-school pageant. Each person looked self-conscious. Some looked scared, some didn't show any emotion at all, some frantically searched the crowd for sight of a loved one. One middle-aged woman began sobbing and blubbering, and she was yanked away instantly.

A slightly dazed-looking Joan was in the door briefly. Her expression was difficult to read. She turned and said something to somebody, presumably Blue Bandanna. She shrugged and left the door.

"That her, Madsen?" Petty said.

"That's her."

The next person was a very old, frail-looking man. When he appeared, Hassie West, his sixty-five-year-old daughter, found that her worst fears had come true. She fainted in the arms of her husband.

You couldn't ask for a better group of hostages than this one. They cut across all social and economic lines in town. From the wealthy to the common laborer, Petty would be getting heat to make a quick, safe deal. Let them have the money. Let them ride away. Plenty of time to go after the outlaws later. Their loved ones were all the townspeople cared about.

And then Tom Rattigan was in the doorway. Blue Bandanna made Rattigan's appearance special. He put the gun right to Rattigan's temple. He opened the door slightly. "You try and rush us or anything like that, he's the first one we kill. You understand that?"

Petty nodded. He sure did understand that. And now he knew there was a very simple way to get Rattigan killed and spare everybody else.

TEN

10:27 a.m.

One of the housekeepers brought news of the bank situation to Caroline Petty. Caroline had been playing the grand piano when the woman — who'd just come from town — rushed into the room excited and out of breath. Caroline had been quite relaxed. Liszt always had that effect on her. There was a mystical quality to his music that made her heady spiritually. Even the girls, without quite understanding why, always requested Liszt when they sat and listened to their mother play.

Her first thought was of Tom. The rest of the situation — the robbers, the hostages, the terrible burden on the town itself — didn't even flit across her mind. *Tom is a hostage.* That was her only thought. *Tom is a hostage.* At first she received this information without any reaction at all. Her mind simply rejected it. *Impossible. Tom isn't a hostage. Hilda is wrong. She gets things wrong constantly. Remember when she told me that the mayor had been struck by a wagon when all that had happened was that he'd been* splashed *by a wagon? She made it sound as if he'd been on his deathbed. This is probably the same thing. Tom can't be a hostage. Things like this don't happen to people like us. Tom is fine. Hilda's just confused is all.*

But then one of the Mexican girls came rushing and said, "Meesus Petty, deed you hear about thee bank?"

And so she sat there on the piano bench, prim, pretty, the ideal woman, one would think, but for her adulterous heart, and this time the news had a catastrophic effect on her. Her mind became a kaleidoscope of terrible images — newspaper and magazine images of bankers lying out in the middle of streets after the shoot-outs were over. Sometimes, the barbaric robbers even managed to do the unthinkable — kill the banker, get the money, and ride off never to be found by the law.

I have to get down there. I can't possibly sit here not knowing how he is. But will Walter suspect something's wrong? Of course not. I can tell him I'm worried about him. It's per-

fectly natural. He's my husband, isn't he? And anyway, why would he suspect that I'm there to see how Tom is? He doesn't know anything about Tom and me. As far as he knows, I hate *Tom for being such a ladies' man. Or at least that's what he* used *to be. Before he met me.*

She got up from the bench. Most days, she put on a pretty dress to go into town. Today, she wore a tight suede rust-colored skirt and a blouse and a sprightly low-brimmed white hat. She would often stand before the mirror in this outfit and note that it made her look a few years younger than she actually was. The skirt displayed her still-firm hips and thighs, while the blouse spoke fetchingly of her breasts. Two children and her breasts were still doing just fine for themselves, thank you.

But today was not most days. Oh, no. Today was not most days at all.

She gave quick instructions to the maid and was gone out the door. She went straight to the barn and rigged up the buggy. She spoke to the chestnut mare. An old friend, this horse. *We need to hurry as never before.*

The scene was a strange one. You could look three blocks down the center of town and not see anybody except her husband

186

and Carney. All the people were crowded along the boardwalks and under the various overhangs. The sun was relentless.

She hitched her horse to a post behind the general store and walked around front to the crowd. Everybody recognized her. They gave her respectful nods, more respectful than usual. A beloved figure she was not. There was a coldness there, an imperiousness that not even all her charity work — you had only to listen to her talk so patronizingly to the poor to know what was in her heart — could disguise her real nature.

There was some talk, but it was mostly whispers, and then only half-sentences and grunts. Nobody wanted to rile anybody up. No telling what bank robbers would do at a time like this. They had to know that their chances for escape were slim. So they'd be all keyed up. The crowd didn't want to cause any trouble by talking too much. Whispers were the order of the day.

Caroline hesitated a moment, looking across the street to the bank. The shade was pulled on the front door. There was nothing to be seen.

"Has anybody been hurt?" she asked.

"Not that I know of, ma'am," said a leather-faced woman in an outsized dress that was made of flour sacks.

"Thank God."

"Yes, ma'am."

It was clear the woman didn't care for her, but right now Caroline didn't give a damn about that. Right now her only concern was Tom.

She walked to the center of the street, her boots stirring up some red dust, and touched her husband's arm.

When he turned and saw who it was, she felt a fear she had never known before in her life. His gaze was filled with unadulterated hatred. And her thought was: *He knows. He knows about Tom and me.*

10:31 a.m.

Molly Rattigan was sitting in her husband's study — the damned man, how could you love and hate a man as much as she did Tom — touching the unloaded pistol he'd used in the Civil War. He always joked that it wasn't much use these days except as a paperweight. That was when the maid said, "There's a policeman here to see you, Mrs. Rattigan."

He was waiting, somber, in the vestibule. She touched long, elegant fingers to her

188

chest and said, "Yes?"

Then she took in his uniform and his awkwardness — he was probably intimidated by the size and splendor of the house, most people were, a fact she liked in some ways (it was fun to play queen), but disliked in others (she really was a pretty down-to-earth person and didn't want people to think otherwise) — and then she took in his somber expression.

"Is everything all right, Officer?"

"Yes, ma'am. I mean, no, ma'am. No, it isn't." He hesitated. "There's been a little trouble at the bank."

The first thing she noticed was the word "little." Whenever people wanted to prepare you for some really bad news, they used words like "little" to diminish the enormity of the problem they were about to present.

"My husband —" she started to say.

"He's fine, ma'am. In fact, we just saw him in the door not long ago."

"The door? What door?"

"The bank door, ma'am."

"What was he doing in the bank door?" She could feel her grip starting to loosen. Anger was in her voice now. Why in God's name had Petty sent such an inarticulate man to give her this message?

"The thing is, ma'am, they're holding him hostage."

"Who are?"

"The robbers."

She was getting it piecemeal, which was the worst way to get it.

"Is he hurt?"

"No, ma'am. He looked fine. You know, in the bank door there."

She said, more to herself than him, "I need to get down there, don't I?"

"I expected you'd want to, ma'am. I brought a buggy. Just in case that's what you decided to do."

She rounded up the maid and told her what was going on. The children were in school. The maid was to pick them up if this thing extended past schooltime. Then she was to make them a snack — the contents of which were up to the maid's discretion — and then to see that the kids got immediately down to their homework. Their father expected much more than Cs and Bs. And take special care of Celia. She's been down again, you know, about her birth defect. (I just don't know what we're going to do about her. I just love her so much and when I see her so sad — I just want to hold her and shut out the world so nobody can ever make fun of her again, the poor little kid.)

And then she was in the buggy with the policeman in his fine uniform. He drove much better than he spoke, maneuvering the buggy down the center of the street, moving fast but not too fast, sitting up straight and looking impressive with his gloves and kepi and sun-sparkling badge.

She experienced the same type of disorientation Caroline Petty had a bit earlier. When you reached town, you expected to see the main street jammed with buggies and wagons and horses and people, especially at this time of day, prime business time. But there was just the hush and the crowd lining the boardwalks on the east side of the street. And in the center Walter Petty and that assistant chief, Carney.

The policeman stashed the buggy, then led her over to Walter Petty. Without saying a word, Petty took her in his arms and held her a long moment. They were social friends. He was playing the protector role, she the role of supplicant. She needed the help of the great white father and by taking her in his arms, he was saying without words that he would indeed help her. Several people in the crowd thought that was a fine thing for the chief to do. He'd succeeded in making Molly Rattigan sympathetic, not always easy to do. Molly was second only to Caroline Petty in her arrogance and disdain for the average person.

"You think Tom's all right?"

"There haven't been any shots fired. And he's their trump card. And they know it."

"The money doesn't matter."

"I know it doesn't. And the money isn't what I'm worried about, Molly."

"Oh? Then what is?"

"Well, the first thing is, I want to get them out of there all right. I don't want anybody hurt at all. But the second thing is, I want to do it in such a way that our little town here doesn't get to be a target for every punk in the Territory."

"I'm not sure what you're saying, Walter."

"I just have to be careful not to look too easy. We don't want this to happen again. If I allow them to ride out of here with a hostage and the money, then every bank robber in the Territory'll come over here to try us out."

"You're saying what exactly, Walter?" Her voice rising, accusatory and irritable now. "You're saying that you'll sacrifice my husband and your friend Tom if need be?"

He put his hand on her shoulder. "C'mon, Molly. Stay calm. I'm not saying that at all."

Her teeth were gritted. Her fingers took his wrist and dug into it. "I don't want him to die, Walt. I don't want him to die."

She had to watch herself. Not say the wrong thing. Petty didn't come from money — a respectable background, yes — but not money. And he was known to be sensitive about any display of class awareness. She wanted to *command* him to take care of her husband. But she didn't dare. He'd get angry, and God only knows what he'd do then. She had to be steady, unemotional. She just thanked the Lord that he didn't know what his wife and her husband were up to. She'd known from the first day of her marriage that Tom needed to run wild sometimes. He always did so discreetly, and he never allowed it to get serious. Oh, she'd found the occasional forgotten love note in his pocket from time to time, but that just reassured her that his flings meant nothing. He eventually broke them all off. Even mistresses can get boring. The notes were invariably pleas from his ladies, pleas that he begin seeing them late at night in this spot or that, pleas that he show the same passion for them that he'd shown at the beginning of the tryst. But no . . . Tom had the original wandering eye. Even a wife and a mistress weren't enough for him — in the middle of one illicit affair he was already looking around for the next one. If he'd loved them, truly loved them, Molly wouldn't have been able to deal with it. But he didn't. And therefore she was safe. She had her husband, whom she would never stop loving, damn the man, anyway, and she had her children and her reputation and her mansion — and why would she throw it all away on some sad woman who thought that Tom Rattigan was in love with her?

She steadied herself. "Please, Walt. Just go easy. Do whatever they want. Please."

He put his hand on her shoulder. "Everything'll be fine, Molly. I know how to handle this."

The crowd was watching her, too. A drama was playing out before them and now all the characters were in place. The tough police chief. His assistant chief, Carney. The banker's wife. Never had a stage melodrama held such fascination for these people. Because they had loved ones or friends in there, too. And they didn't have to be told how often something like this turned into a bloodbath. Their stomachs burned, their fingers twitched, tics appeared in the corners of their eyes, sphincters tightened, and breaths came shallow and fast. God, oh, God, please, no bloodbaths here. That was most people, anyway. Of course there were a few who *wanted* to see bloodshed. Oh, they'd tell you how awful it was, all those lives wasted that way, but secretly, secretly the spectacle of a true bloodbath would be exciting to watch in a way that was almost sexual. They'd never admit it — maybe not even to themselves — but that was the God's truth. Watching people die would give them a real and undeniable thrill.

She detached herself from Walt and Carney and walked back toward the crowd. At first, she wasn't sure where she was headed exactly, but then it became clear that she was going over to stand by Caroline Petty. The two women were friends, the most prominent duo of society ladies in the entire Territory. The best-looking, the most sought-out by the newspapers, the most dreamt-about by scruffy young men who liked to walk by the big mansions and dream of everything that went on inside those houses — the meals, the evenings before the open fires, the sex

. . . oh, yes, the sex . . . that went on in those boudoirs (to use that French word for bedroom) . . . oh, yes, the sex.

She didn't say a word to Caroline. There was nothing *to* say. The situation being so obvious and all.

But she did fall into Caroline's open arms and let Caroline hold her and comfort her and even rock her a little. The funny thing was — even though this was the whore who was sleeping with her husband — it wasn't at all unpleasant in these arms. If Caroline hadn't been such a slut, Molly would have been able to appreciate her for the generous, sweet, intelligent person Caroline was most of the time. Having affairs wasn't like her. She was both a good mother and wife. She had married Walt without ever falling in love with him — Molly suspected Caroline had never really fallen in love with anyone (she'd been a terribly sheltered girl) until she began having her nights with Tom. She almost couldn't blame her old friend. There were fates worse than death and one of them was named Walter Petty.

The crowd liked seeing the two women embrace this way. Made the rich bitches human. Showed that when you took away the fancy dresses and the uppity way of speaking and the barely disguised scorn for the average people, what you had were two pretty ordinary and probably pretty decent women who were worried about their husbands and their children just the way common folks were.

"It's going to be all right," Caroline said gently as she let Molly move free of her arms. "Walt's a very good policeman. He knows how to handle situations like this."

Oh, I hope so, Molly thought. Because otherwise the man both of us love could get himself killed.

Then they faced front and started staring at the bank the way everybody else was. They sure wished they knew what was going on inside there.

10:47 a.m.

"I want half of you over here and the other half over there."

Leonard really did wonder sometimes why his brother Karl was considered the smart one. In terms of book reading and things of that nature, Karl no doubt had the edge. But book learning had its limitations. He'd met a lot of book-learned people who didn't know jackshit about regular normal practical everyday life. And that went for other things, too, where Karl was concerned. Leonard could screw longer, drink more, punch harder, and piss farther than Karl could any day of the week. Plus which, Karl had his moods. He was almost like a girl when he got into his moods. This big, sad look on his face. And barely able to talk. Or — from what Leonard could tell — think clearly.

For instance. After bringing each hostage to the door, Karl wanted them to lie down on the floor again. And that just didn't make any sense at all now, did it? Suppose the lawmen rushed the front or back doors? What good were hostages lying on the floor? You needed hostages standing upright so you could put them in front of you as a shield. There wouldn't be time to bend down and pick somebody up like that.

So it was Leonard who had to figure it out.

"You, there. And you, over here. And you — why you patting your pocket all the time? Turn that pocket inside out. Let me see what's in there."

The man nervously turned it inside out. Leonard kept his gun on him. The pocket was empty. "Over there, then."

And so on.

And what was brother Karl doing all this time? Standing over in the corner looking forlorn as hell, the hostage of one of his moods. He didn't have his gun drawn. He had already given in to the notion that it was all over for them, that they had two choices — die in a blaze of bullets or give themselves up. But Leonard wasn't about to give in to either fate. He planned to get out of this town with both the money and his freedom.

One of the women started crying then. She leaned toward the guard, as if she were going to put her head on his shoulder.

Leonard stepped over to her and slapped her. The flat of his hand created a sound that filled the bank. It carried a savage edge that startled everybody. It shocked the woman out of crying. She looked too stunned — and too scared — to cry. "I told you no physical contact."

"I hope I get my hands on you," the guard said.

"I like feisty old men, Gramps," Leonard smiled. "I'm proud of you for sticking up for her. But right now, I want you to keep your mouth shut. You understand?"

The guard just glowered at him.

Leonard looked over his work. Good. One half of the people against one wall of the bank, the other half against the facing wall. And Leonard in the middle with his gun.

He smiled at his brother. "We kill El Presidente here first." He nodded to Rattigan.

"Shut up, Leonard," Karl said. "We're not killing anybody."

"Maybe you aren't, brother. But if I need to — I am." His anger became a cold smile. "We've had disagreements all our life. Some brothers are like that. Ma and Pa always said you was the smart one and the pretty one and the good one — while me, well, I was just a little runt they didn't care much for. Just kind of a tagalong." Then he turned the chill smile on his brother. "I want your gun, brother."

"What the hell're you talking about?" Karl said.

"You're acting funny. I think you're scared. And I don't need that right now. I'm planning to get away from here, even if you're not." He nodded to Karl's gun belt. "So you just set your gun down on the floor real nice and easy, Karl, and then you get over here with the rest of the people."

"You're my damn brother, Leonard," Karl said in clear exasperation. "What the hell you think you're doing?"

"I don't trust you is what I'm doing. You're starting to cave in on me, brother, and that scares the hell out of me. I plan to get away from here even if you don't."

Karl still acted as if this was some kind of prank. "Leonard, do you know how stupid this is? *I'm your brother.*"

"Stupid? That's what you've been calling me all my life, Karl. Now put your gun on the floor or —"

"Or what?" Karl was fully awake now and out of his mood. Completely focused on this crazy scene with his little brother.

"Or else I'll shoot you."

Karl made a face and glanced at the hostages. They were enjoying this, no doubt. What hostage wouldn't love to see his captors arguing with each other? "You realize this is just what they want, don't you?"

Leonard turned in time to see a few smirks on the faces of the hostages. They thought this was so damned funny.

He said, "You won't be laughing when I start killing you off one by one."

The smirks disappeared.

He raised his gun, turned at an angle, and pointed it directly at his brother's heart. "You got your choice, Karl. You lay your gun down or I kill you right here. You're not tough enough to do what needs to be done. I'm sorry it's got to be this way, but it has to. Now you make up your mind. I think you know I'm not slinging any bullshit. I'll drop you right where you stand."

The quiet way Leonard spoke — it was usually bluster — and the steady way he held his gun started to convince Karl that Leonard had finally found something like pride within himself. He just might go ahead and kill his older brother in cold blood. And if he had any regrets, they'd probably come a long, long time after.

Karl said, "I'm putting my gun down, Leonard."

"I'm sure glad you saw it my way, brother."

Karl couldn't believe how poised and tender Leonard sounded at this moment. It was as if Karl was no longer dealing with his brother but with an imposter.

11:03 a.m.

A middle-aged man led an elderly blind woman up on the boardwalk near where Madsen stood. The girl next to Madsen said, "She's the grandmother of one of the women inside."

The grief was oppressive. So was the growing fear that this situation would not end well. If the robbers hadn't surrendered by now . . .

Madsen walked down into the street. Carney saw him coming and frowned. He whispered something to Chief Petty. His frown grew deeper.

"I believe the chief told you to wait on the boardwalk with the rest of the folks," Carney said when Madsen reached him.

Petty didn't even look at Madsen. He just stared straight at the bank. Madsen was too insignificant to look at, apparently.

"I'm a priest," Madsen said. "I'm used to talking to troubled people. I'd like to talk to the robbers if I could."

Carney said, "This is a police operation here. We don't need no priest. Now you get back there with everybody else."

"Is he speaking for you, too, Chief?"

Petty looked at him. "You're beginning to irritate me, Mr. Madsen. Or Father Madsen. Whichever it is. Haven't I got a big problem on my hands here? Now you do what Carney says. You get back on that boardwalk and you stay there."

"You heard the chief," Carney said. "Now git." He was uneasy talking to anybody this way — he rarely did — but he felt he needed to impress Walt with his toughness. So he flung his arm out the way he would with a dog he was setting in a particular direction. "And I don't want to hear another peep from you, either."

Madsen went back to the boardwalk, and Caroline Petty and Molly Rattigan walked down to where he was standing. Caroline said, "I understand you're a priest."

Madsen nodded and introduced himself.

"Have you ever dealt with situations like this?" she asked.

"A couple of times there was a Pima standoff. I helped get everybody to settle down. Nobody got hurt, at any rate."

"I saw you talking to my husband. Does he know you're a priest?"

"I told him. I'm not sure he believes me. The first time I saw him I was wearing a gun."

"Did you offer your services just now?"

He wondered why she was so anxious, so nervous. Her husband was in control of the situation. He'd be fine. Then he thought, maybe she has a relative in the bank.

"Yes, I did."

"And he said no?"

"He said he could handle it."

"That's just like him," she said. It

sounded like a curse, the sharp, angry way she said it. Then she seemed embarrassed, as if she'd revealed far more about herself — and her marriage — than she'd intended. "I'm going to go up and talk to him."

"I don't think it'll do you any good."

"I don't want anybody killed."

"I'm sure nobody does, ma'am." But he actually wasn't sure about that. He didn't sense any great resolve on Petty's part to settle this peacefully.

"I'll be back, Molly," she said to the watery-eyed, pale woman next to her. "I'm sure Father Madsen here will help you out if you need anything."

11:17 a.m.

"Here comes your missus," Carney said.

Petty almost smiled. She'd have a hard time just standing there on the boardwalk — not doing anything — while her lover boy was in the hands of the robbers. This pleased Petty, it really did. He wondered if she'd ever be able to fathom the pain and humiliation he'd felt standing on the edge of the clearing seeing her in that gazebo with Rattigan. Whatever she was going through now was nothing; nothing.

"Why don't you see how the other boys are doing?" Petty said. Meaning he wanted to be alone with Caroline. Carney understood, gave him his little half-ass salute, and departed to check on the other policemen.

Caroline came up next to him and said, "I was just talking with Father Madsen."

"You really think he's a priest? I'm not so sure of that. Don't let him take you in."

"Why would he lie?"

"Maybe he's a confidence man. A Roman collar makes a nice hiding place."

"He wants to talk to the robbers. He says he helped out a few times when there was trouble with the Pimas."

Petty smiled. "Caroline, think about it. What's he going to say to them that *I* can't say? If these were good religious boys, that'd be one thing. They might listen to him. But these boys are bank robbers. And they take hostages, which is a pretty low thing to do, one of the lowest, in fact. So what's a priest — if he really is a priest — going to say that moves them one way or the other? Nothing. Nothing at all."

"So you're going to do what, Walter? Just wait until they do something so you

206

can rush the bank and get half the people in there killed?"

The smile again. But not the nice, warm smile of good old Walter. This was the cold smile of odd, angry Walter, Walter the Stranger. This was the smile — and the man — who frightened her. "If I didn't know any better, I'd think you have a loved one in that bank. You have a loved one in there, do you, Caroline?"

Her blush was her true answer. But she said, "I'm just concerned for the towns-people, is all."

"I see." He wanted to say more — he wanted to blurt out everything he knew and shame her — but he couldn't afford to. Not with what he had in mind. "You better get back there, Caroline. Molly's going to need you. You left her with Madsen, didn't you?"

She nodded. She was starting to cry.

"Well, he won't be anywhere near the comfort you will. You better get back there and help her. She's got a husband in there, you know. Good old Tom Rattigan." The ironic way he said Tom's name was taking a risk, and he immediately said, "Tom's my friend, too, remember. I sure don't want to get him killed."

He could feel her eyes on him. It was almost as if she knew that he knew about her and Tom. She just wanted to see it in his face.

"Go on and help Molly out, honey," he said.

And she went on her way.

He faced the bank again. The time was now for getting it all rolling. He needed to get Carney here and tell him what to do. He was sure glad Carney was reasonably sober.

11:33 a.m.

Chief Walter Petty realized that before he gave Carney his instructions, he had to pretend to try to resolve the situation peacefully. He was known as a temperate man. He didn't want that impression to change. He hoped to be mayor someday, and who knows after that. In the West, some lawmen, those who kept themselves above reproach, did well in politics. And he was tired of being seen as an earnest but somewhat plodding man by his wealthy in-laws. He wanted to show them that earnest was not a bad thing, and plodding was sometimes the correct pace in reaching one's goal. A lot of fast starters littered the sides of the road.

He'd spent several minutes sipping coffee and rehearsing his words. The coffee had come courtesy of The Miner's Café. Every half hour or so one of the girls from there brought him a fresh cup.

Finally he felt ready. He was no ham — or if he was, wasn't aware of it, at any rate — so this sort of thing didn't come easily to him.

He began by holding his six-shooter up in the air and saying to the blank face of the bank, "I want you to see that I'm laying down my guns." He then leaned down and set the six-shooter in the dust. (The dramatic way he did it, maybe there was some ham in him after all.) Then he took the rifle that had been leaning against his leg and did likewise. "Now I'm unarmed. And I'm going to take a few steps forward. I just hope you're not crazy enough to shoot me."

He could feel the crowd's pulse quicken now. This was real drama. Petty might be a stuffy asshole sometimes, but there was no denying he was a first-rate lawman.

He took a few steps forward. But instead of lowering his voice, as he'd said he wanted to, he raised it. He wanted the crowd to hear him loud and clear.

"I have a proposition to make with you. I'll exchange myself for Tom Rattigan, the president of the bank. He's worth a lot as a hostage, but I'm worth even more because I'm the chief of police."

He knew damned well they wouldn't do this. You start exchanging hostages that way, you started losing control of everything. And you open that door and everything go could wrong at once.

"This has gone on long enough. There are elderly people in there who can't hold up under the strain of this. I don't want them to get sick — or worse. So you take me as your hostage and take your money and ride out of here. That way nobody but me gets hurt."

He paused. He sensed that his words were effective, but he felt a little self-conscious. He was standing in the middle of an empty, heat-blasted street talking to a shade-drawn bank.

"You don't have to decide now. But you've only got fifteen minutes to make your mind up. I know how these things work. The longer you're in the bank there, the more likely somebody's going to get killed. I'm not going to let that happen. I'm going to end this in the next fifteen minutes. You understand me?"

The door opened then. Maybe an inch. The voice this time was different. This time it was Red, not Blue, Bandanna.

"The bank president is fine with me. I'm not interested in swapping. You know damned well it's just some kind of trick you got in mind. Now in fifteen minutes, I'm walking out of here with Rattigan, and you're gonna have a horse ready for me and him and we're gonna ride away."

Petty wanted to ask about the other one, the one in the blue kerchief, but he knew this wasn't the time. He said, "I can't let you take one of our citizens away like that. That's why I say I'm willing to be your hostage. That's my job; not Tom Rattigan's."

"Well, you know what you can do with your job, mister. You just have that horse ready because in fifteen minutes, I'm comin' out with Rattigan."

The bank door slammed.

Petty completed his performance well. He allowed his shoulders to slump, and when he turned around to walk back to his weapons, he looked up at the crowd just once so they could see his pensive and sad face. And he shook his head. A lot of worry and weariness went into that head shake. And as he glanced at his fellow citizens, he saw that just about every one of them regarded him with admiration.

He was damned well relieved was what he was. What if that crazy sonofabitch had actually taken him up on his offer? Most bank robbers were lifelong criminals. And wouldn't a hardened criminal just love to have a police chief as a hostage? Rattigan probably had an even chance of surviving. The outlaws might just run him out to the foothills, dump him, and take off on their own. Two men could make a lot better time than three men. But there was no way Petty would survive. Not a chance.

He took up his lonely position in front of the bank. Now everything was set up for Carney to go to work.

And just as he had thought, he saw Carney walking toward him. Good old Carney. He'd be very happy when Petty told him what he wanted him to do.

"Everybody's at their post," Carney said. "Just waiting around to see what happens, I guess, same as we are."

"We're going to make something happen, Carney."

"We are?"

"Longer they have those hostages, the more likely they'll start killing people. We're going to force their hand."

"How we going to do that?"

"I'm going to lay it all out for you, Carney. Right now."

11:41 a.m.

It was clear to Madsen that Petty had a definite plan of action in mind. He talked to Carney intensely, pointing here and there as he spoke. Madsen knew there was no point in trying to talk to Petty again.

"You get up on that roof and shoot through the side window," Petty was saying to Carney. "One of the robbers is bound to walk in front of it. Wait him out. Then kill him."

Carney looked as if he hadn't understood. "But if I kill one of the robbers, Chief, the other one will kill Tom Rattigan for sure. He's your friend, Chief."

A sour expression worked across Petty's grim face. "I tell you I'm going to give you your job back and what's the first thing you do — you argue about the orders I give you. If you don't want to do this, Red, then I'll find somebody who will."

But Petty knew what the answer would be. Red sure didn't want to have to go home and tell his wife he didn't have a job.

All Madsen could do was watch Carney. Petty would stay out in front of the bank to negotiate. Carney was the one who would set the plan in motion. There was little hope that the robbers would surrender anything now. They knew that exchanging Petty for Rattigan was a ruse of some kind.

The people seemed to realize this, too. There was almost no small talk now. Especially among the people with loved ones inside. Something was going to happen. They had to agree with Petty. The longer a hostage situation went, the more people who died — usually, anyway. There was always the hope that this incident would be the exception. But most of them knew better.

Nearing noon, the sun was without mercy. Petty's face gleamed with sweat as he talked with Carney. Some of the female onlookers had paper fans. They used them on themselves and on some of the older folks.

Nothing happened to the front door of the bank. The doorknob didn't rattle, the shade didn't go up, the pane of glass didn't shake. Everybody knew his business. Petty was waiting for his time limit to expire.

The robbers were waiting to see what Petty would do. And the crowd was here to watch helplessly.

Carney broke away from Petty. Nothing dramatic. Nothing that would make anybody think he was up to anything in particular. Just broke away with his carbine and started walking down the street away from the bank. There were two buildings before the next cross street. When he came to this street, he turned right and was quickly out of sight.

Madsen looked at the two buildings on the other side of the alley from the bank. When he'd gone around back of the bank, he'd seen the long, narrow window on the side of the place. There was an alley's worth of distance between the bank window and the side of the next building. A man could get on the roof of the facing building and have himself a good shot into the bank. If one of the robbers happened to be in that window — and given the fact that it was at least five feet tall, narrowed and arched, there was probably no shade to be drawn — he could kill the robber without much trouble at all.

This was the plan.

Madsen knew that Petty would see him if he went down the street. He needed to get in the alley on the buildings behind him, then take the long way around — maybe four blocks away before crossing over to the bank side of the street — so Petty couldn't see him.

He had to hurry.

11:56 a.m.

Caroline just kept remembering the look on Walt's face when she'd first walked up to him. *He knew about the affair she was having with Tom.* That fact was there to be seen in the controlled rage of his gaze. *He knew.* And, she sensed, he was going to do something about it, too.

She needed to warn Tom. Somehow. Some way.

Molly said, "Are you all right, Caroline? Look at your hands."

Caroline forced a smile. "I'm supposed to be comforting you, remember. It's just this whole — situation. I just don't want to see anybody hurt is all. I don't have the steadiest nerves, I'm afraid." She clasped her hands together to still their shaking.

Molly watched her carefully. *She knows.* Once again, Caroline had that same sense — that her secret wasn't a secret. That the person staring at her knew all about her affair with Tom. But she was being silly. And if she was being silly about Molly . . . maybe she was being silly about Walt. Maybe guilt — as much as she loved Tom and wanted him to run away with her, she'd hardly escaped guilt, getting on her hands and knees every night and morning and asking God to understand her and forgive her for the terribly selfish thing she was about to do — maybe guilt was playing tricks on her. Maybe Walt didn't know anything about her affair with Tom at all.

"I've never prayed so hard in my life," Molly said.

"Neither have I. And thanks for being concerned about me."

Again that peculiar, knowing look in Molly's eyes. It was the heat. The desperate situation. The guilt. All of it combining to make her think that Molly knew. If Caroline didn't get hold of herself, she'd soon be imagining that everybody in town knew. Hadn't she read a Poe story like that in boarding school? Where a man lost his mind because he started believing that everybody knew his terrible secret?

Had to get hold of herself; had to. She straightened up. Patted her hair. Gave

Molly a hug. Saw Molly scan the street. And look disappointed.

Molly said, "I wonder where Carney went to. I just hope Walt doesn't force their hands. You know what a hothead Carney is. He loves stirring up violence."

"Walt's a sensible man," she said, defending her husband. "He won't do anything to get anybody hurt." *If only I believed that, then I could relax, too.*

"I just hope you're right," Molly Rattigan said anxiously, "I just hope you're right."

ELEVEN

12:07 p.m.

There was a screened back door. Madsen opened it and went inside. The building had two floors. A stairway led to the floor above. Madsen assumed this was where Carney had gone.

Madsen went up the stairs on tiptoe. The building was silent. Everybody would be outside, watching the events at the bank. By now the whole thing had taken on the elevated importance of a religious pageant. Unfortunately, the ending of this particular ritual wasn't known as yet.

The second-floor hall was empty, too. It smelled of light dust and sunlight streaming through a front window. The four office doors were closed. When Madsen looked behind him he saw the ladder. The rungs didn't start until two feet off the ground. They climbed to the

219

ceiling and a trapdoor. The door was open and he could see a square of blue sky. Carney was up there. With his rifle.

Madsen jumped on the steps and climbed up. When he came near the top, he put his head through the opening and looked around. Carney was on one knee, aiming his rifle out and down the side window of the bank.

Madsen eased himself up on the noisy tin roof. Quiet as he moved, Carney heard him. Turned, saw him. Stood up. Started walking toward him. "What the hell you doing up here, mister? Now get the hell back down on the street where you belong."

"You shoot into the bank that way, you're going to get people killed. You'll panic the robbers and they'll just start shooting the hostages."

"I don't see the badge you're wearing, mister. Can't seem to recall you being on the police payroll."

"It just stands to reason."

"And you're up here to do what exactly? Stop me?"

"If I can. But I'd rather try and reason with you."

"Why don't you try and reason with the robbers?"

"I'd like to but your chief of police won't let me." Carney was near him now. Sweaty, stinking of alcohol. The sunlight had gone a long ways toward sobering him up. "You must have friends in the bank. People you've known all your life, if you're from around here. You want to get them killed? Your chief isn't infallible, you know. He might be a smart man, but even smart men can make mistakes. He's worried about setting an example of these two so other robbers won't get the same idea about coming here. But what's the point of setting an example if you just get a lot of people killed in the process?"

Carney sighed. "You know something? Now I believe you're a priest. You sound like a priest. And I'm a Catholic. Used to be an altar boy, long time ago." He smiled. "Always tripping over the cassock I had to wear. It was always too long for me till I got to be around twelve or so. So what I'm saying is that I understand your concern, Father. I really do. But the chief thinks this is the best way to handle things and I tend to agree. And I don't have any choice. I got to obey his orders, Father."

"You don't look happy."

"Sometimes you have to do things you don't want to, I guess. Now, please, Father;

221

please don't get me in trouble. I'm fighting to keep my job here. I'm sorry. But that's the way it's got to be."

He dismissed Madsen by turning around and walking back to his post. He must have been convinced that his words had had the desired effect because he didn't even check to see if Madsen had actually left the roof. He hadn't. He stood in the heat — up there on the tin roof, feeling as if a giant magnifying glass were being held close to him, doubling the sun's effects — trying to think of what to do next.

Obviously, he wasn't going to change Carney's mind. And he didn't have a gun to put in Carney's back. The only thing he could do was —

But he didn't have to worry about his plan because it was just then that Carney looked over his shoulder and saw Madsen.

He turned around, still on his haunches, and said, "Father, please. Now just get back downstairs. Please."

Madsen didn't have any choice but to comply. He couldn't think of a reason to stay up there, and he didn't have any way of forcing Carney to put his rifle down and give up on this stupid idea.

He nodded silently to Carney and went back down the ladder. When he reached the ground floor he went into the alley and found what he was looking for. He grabbed it and hurried back inside. A few minutes later, he was peering through the opening in the roof. Carney was just starting to sight along his rifle. Madsen had to hurry.

There was no way he could get close to Carney. The tin roof made that impossible. Even on tiptoe a man made a lot of noise. He'd have to try it from very near the hatch itself. It was a long way to throw. Madsen had been a number of things in his life, but a baseball pitcher wasn't one of them.

But what choice did he have? He had to prevent what he knew would be a disaster from happening.

The rock he'd picked up filled his hand. It was dirty and dusty and had a few sharp edges on it. If he could hit Carney in the back of the head, the man would be out cold for a while. No doubt about it.

He took aim. He aimed with one eye, then two eyes, then one eye again. He said an Our Father. He didn't want to do serious injury to Carney.

And then he let fly.

At first, the arc of the rock was disappointing. It looked as if it would land a few inches to the side of Carney's head. But as the rock began to fall, its course altered just enough so that when it struck, it didn't hit Carney's shoulder but the back of his head. The blow was hard enough to knock Carney down. He pitched right, his rifle falling from his hands. Madsen wanted to make sure Carney was all right — and he wanted to take Carney's rifle. He moved so quickly there were loud, metallic tramping noises on the sun-glaring tin roof.

He slowed down as he got closer. He remembered from his war days that a fallen man was not necessarily an unconscious one. He approached cautiously. Carney didn't move. Or moan. Madsen had a terrible moment thinking that he might have killed the man. He'd had mixed feelings about hurling the stone, anyway. Was that something he should be doing given the vows he'd taken? But what choice had he had? Firing into the bank would rile up the robbers. People would die. There was no doubt about that. Petty was a smart man. He obviously could reason it out for himself. So therefore the question had to be: *Why did Petty want the robbers to start shooting in retaliation? Clearly something was going on here that Madsen wasn't able to understand. Even a tinhorn lawman wouldn't make this mistake, even if he did want to make an example of this duo and send a message to any future bandits.*

Carney was snake-quick. His hand lashed out and grabbed Madsen by the ankle. Carney was powerful enough to yank the larger man to his back on the tin roof. And then Carney was up and furious. He started by kicking Madsen in the ribs several times, then fell on Madsen and started smashing his fist into the priest's face. Blood pooled in Madsen's nostrils and spilled down the front of his lips and jaw. Madsen was a strong adversary, though. He seized one of Carney's wrists and twisted it so hard, Carney was afraid he'd broken it. This gave the bigger man time to grab Carney by one shoulder and toss him off.

Madsen leapt to his feet, ready as Carney, also on his feet, grabbed for the Winchester. Madsen hurled himself at the other man, pushing him away from the weapon. Carney returned the favor. As Madsen made a grab for the rifle, Carney came at him with an uppercut that pushed Madsen back three feet. Then it was Madsen's turn again. As Carney stooped to snap the weapon up, Madsen grabbed him by the hair and jerked away so hard,

Carney's face disintegrated into pure pain.

But he fooled Madsen. The moment Madsen let go of his hair, Carney feinted to the left and then dove for the Winchester. This time he got it, and quickly pushed the muzzle of it about a quarter inch from Madsen's bloody face.

"Father, I just don't know what the hell to do with you." He was still gasping for air. "I know you shouldn't hurt a priest, but you just don't leave me any choice."

Carney had the stone now. He bounced it up and down in his palm. "You've got good taste in rocks, Padre. This is a nice one."

"I'm glad you appreciate my taste in rocks. You going to use that on me?"

"You're a smart one. I've got to give you that." He bounced it up and down a few more times. "You didn't hurt me all that bad. You clipped me more than anything."

"You'll be a little luckier, I imagine."

Carney bounced the rock a couple more times and said, "Turn around, Father. That'll make this easier for both of us. I'll try not to hurt you much. I really will."

"What if I *don't* turn around?"

"Then I guess I hit you in the forehead, Father. It's my job or I wouldn't do it."

Then he did it. And Madsen sank to the scorching tin roof, unconscious.

12:17 p.m.

Joan was standing three feet from Karl Schmitt when the first bullet shattered the glass of the bank's side window.

The bullet entered Karl's forehead just above his left eyebrow. The second bullet tore off a good deal of his front scalp.

Joan was sprayed with a hot mixture of blood, bone, and hair. The way she jerked about, flinging herself against the wall, an onlooker might surmise that she, too, had been shot. In fact, her sustained scream was louder than Karl's brief one.

Karl was lifted from the floor by a good three inches and slammed into the wall very near where Joan was. Unlike Joan, Karl left several whorls and splashes of blood on the wall. A bloody tuft of hair adhered to the wallpaper and stayed there.

Karl had been an easy and obvious target for Carney. Karl had left his bandanna on. He had no gun — his brother Leonard had taken that earlier — but that point was moot, anyway. A gun wouldn't have done him any good against a sniper attack from the roof.

The most interesting person to watch in the first moments following the shooting was Leonard Schmitt.

He had to hold not only himself but his hostages together. If there was a moment when he might lose control, this was it. He had to assimilate three key facts at once: 1) that his brother had been assassinated; 2) that the pretty girl who'd been going to kill Rattigan might have been shot, too; and 3) that Rattigan was already running to the door and flinging it open. Leonard was at his back in moments, but not before Rattigan pulled the door open and screamed: "Are you insane, Petty? Are you trying to get us killed in here?" In his own panic, Rattigan hadn't thought of escaping — merely pleading with the police chief to act sensibly.

Leonard grabbed Rattigan, slammed the door shut, then pushed Rattigan to the middle of the bank floor with the others. Two or three of them had moved from their previous positions. Dickens, the bank guard, was halfway to the back door. Obviously, they'd thought of trying to escape. But the shock of Karl's gory death and the lack of time had ended any hope of it.

Only after everybody was back in place did Leonard drop to one knee next to his brother and look over the corpse. He made no sound whatsoever. Once he started to touch the man's face — the blue bandanna was still in place — but he stopped himself. Then he made a quick, almost cursory, sign of the cross. The tears came immediately after. His eyes gleamed with them, and for a time he looked dazed as he climbed to unsteady legs.

He stood like this for two full minutes. The hostages began looking back and forth at each other. What was going on? Why hadn't he said anything? Why hadn't he done anything? The eyes were dry now, the legs steady again.

He seemed to be consciously making plans. That was the only thing they could imagine him doing. If he'd been grieving, certainly he would have given some kind of sign.

Finally, he spoke. The bully sound of him was gone. A few of them even had trouble understanding the words he spoke so softly. "All of you but Rattigan, get on out of here. One at a time. Out the front door. And I mean right now." He waved his gun at them, but angled it toward the front door.

They seemed not to understand. They looked baffled. As if he had just told them some truth so profound that it completely poleaxed them mentally and emotionally. *Get out of here now. One at a time. The front door*. What could such arcane words possibly mean?

And then their expressions changed after the moments of bafflement. Oh, yes, the front door. *My God, he was letting them go.*

Then it didn't take long at all. The men were gentlemen. Though they reached the front door before the women, they stood aside to let the ladies through first. Just in case the robber had some trick in mind and was going to detain a few of them at the last moment. But he didn't detain them. He stood near the teller cages. Rattigan stood nearby. Rattigan was soaked with sweat now. He was down to his expensive white shirt and trousers. God knows where his vest and jacket had gone.

"I'm only gonna take one bag of that money," Leonard said. "It's all I can carry."

Rattigan actually smiled. "You think I give a damn about the money now? Your brother's lying there with half his head shot off and you're going to use me as a shield — and you expect me to care about the money? Take all of it if you can carry it. Hell, I held back some. There's more in a small trapdoor in the bottom of the vault. You can take that, too, for all I care. I want to see my wife and daughters. That's all I give a shit about now. You know what a port-wine stain is? It's this purple birthmark. And some people get it on their face. My youngest daughter has it. A beautiful girl except for that. I'm the best friend she's got in the whole world. And I'm not just saying that. That's the truth. I'm scared to die, mister. I'm not going to bullshit you there. Right now — well, I'm just lucky I haven't shit my pants and thrown up all over this floor. And my legs are shaking so bad they feel like they'll give out any time. But you know what's even worse — and this is the God's truth — it's thinking that I might not be around to help my daughter get through life. She's so ashamed of herself. She's the only person that I've ever been able to love. I want to be around her. I just hope you can understand that."

But Leonard's eyes and voice were pitiless. "All I understand is my brother's over there dead. Some sonofabitch shot him for no good reason at all. He didn't kill nobody. Why'd they have to kill him?"

"That bastard Petty. The chief of police. I don't know *what* the hell he's trying to do. I'm sorry about your brother. I really am." Then, softly: "What're you going to do?"

231

Leonard had been staring at his brother's corpse again. The scalp looked worse than if an Indian warrior had had at it with a knife. His eyes lifted to meet Rattigan's. "I guess we're going to find out, aren't we?"

12:23 p.m.

By the time Madsen got back to the boardwalk with the crowd, he sensed a different mood on the street. The people seemed more relaxed now, little more than spectators. He didn't sense tension, just curiosity.

He was wondering what had brought this about when somebody slipped an arm through his and said, "I've been looking for you."

Joan said this in a flat voice. She was pale. He sensed something had shaken her. "Could we go somewhere and talk, Father?" He noticed the unmistakable stains of blood sprayed across her blue gingham dress.

"Sure."

She looked at his face. "Have you been in a fight?"

"Sort of." But he didn't offer any further explanation.

A block down, there was a hotel with a roof over the porch. They sat in the shade.

"You know why I came here."

He nodded. "And that's why *I* came here. To stop you."

"I came pretty close to doing it. I was in his office holding a gun on him when those robbers came in. I would've killed him if they hadn't shown up." She paused. And let out a long, ragged sigh. "One of the robbers got killed a little while ago."

"So he did it after all."

"Who?"

"The chief's man. His name is Carney."

"How do you know it was this Carney who fired that shot?"

"We had a fight up on the roof. Then he knocked me out."

Joan nodded. "They were brothers — the robbers, I mean. I actually felt sorry for the man. For both of them. The one who died and his brother."

"Is that where you got all that blood?"

"I was standing close to him when he got shot." She hesitated. "I never saw a man shot before, Father." She hesitated again. "Now I'm glad I didn't kill Rattigan. Even with everything he did to my father —" She played with the hands in her lap. "I'm glad I didn't kill him."

"I'm glad you didn't, either." Then: "How did you get out of the bank?"

"The robber let us go. Just walked out. Everybody except Rattigan."

"Rattigan's his best hole card, there's no doubt about that. He'll be using him as a shield very soon now."

"There wasn't any reason to kill that man."

"No, there wasn't."

"But they'll get away with it because they're law. Just like the law that put my father in prison." Her bitterness gave her face a strained, older look.

"There's something going on with that chief of police."

"Something going on?"

"The way he's handled all this. Hostage situations go on for a long time sometimes. Sometimes, the longer they go, people get killed. But patience never hurts. I don't know what his hurry was. He forced a showdown and that makes me wonder why."

"Maybe it's just the way he is. Some lawmen take everything personally. That marshal that arrested my father —"

"There's something else. Something personal, I'd guess."

"Like what?"

He shrugged. "I wish I knew."

His eyes narrowed, took in Main Street. "That's why everybody seems more re-laxed now. The hostages are all free."

"What'll happen next?"

"The robber'll try and get out of there."

"Petty'll never let him. Maybe he'll give himself up."

"I don't think Petty'll let him do that, ei-ther." His jaws locked. He watched as Carney came up from the far end of the street and stood next to Petty. "They want bloodshed. Petty and Carney."

She said, "You know the funny thing, Father?"

"What?"

"Now I don't want to see him killed. Rattigan, I mean."

"I'm glad you said that, Joan."

"I had doubts, anyway. When I got to town, I started asking around about him. He's got this daughter who's got this birthmark all over the left side of her face. People told me that he loves her so much she's practically his whole life." She looked at her hands in her lap again. "It isn't fair."

"What isn't?"

"That somebody like Rattigan would love

somebody like his daughter the way he does."

"What's unfair about it?"

A faint, odd smile touched her lips. "Because I wanted him to be a bad man through and through. I want to believe in bad and good. It's too confusing otherwise." She paused. "He sent my father to prison. And he really did cost him his life. But then he turns around and loves his poor little daughter that way — I just wanted him to be a — a . . ."

He laughed. "It's all right, Joan. You can say the word if you want."

"A sonofabitch. That's what I wanted him to be. A sonofabitch and nothing else. No poor little daughter. No being so protective of her and gentle with her and —"

He stood up. Walked to the steps of the hotel. Peered down the street. Just then Petty started talking to the bank again. From here, you couldn't make out the words clearly. But there was a definite sense that everything was heading to a climax, especially since Carney was reloading his Winchester.

"I don't want to see anybody else get killed, Father," she said to Madsen's back, getting up from her porch chair.

"Neither do I," he said.

They were walking back to the crowd when the old priest came out of an alley. He moved slowly in the sun, like an ancient leathered animal indigenous to the desert. His Aztec features were brutal in the hard sunlight. Only the complex, enigmatic darkness of his gaze suggested empathy. He held up a greeting hand.

"I've prayed for them," the old priest said, his hand indicating the standoff. He nodded to Joan. "You people were at early Mass the last three mornings."

"Yes, Father. The Mexican women sing very well," Madsen said.

"A mixture of ancient tongues — Latin and Spanish," the old priest said. "I understand that one of the bandits was killed."

"Yes," Madsen said. "Now his brother is in there with Rattigan the banker."

"Mr. Rattigan," the priest said, brushing dust from his threadbare cassock. He smiled. "Maybe God can figure him out. Nobody else can seem to."

"I grew up with him in an orphanage. We couldn't figure him out, either."

The old priest nodded toward the crowd. "Why did they need to kill him?"

"They didn't," Madsen said.

"That isn't like Petty. He is usually a very calm man. He doesn't use violence unless he needs to. He's very good at talking people out of it, in fact."

"We're walking down there," Madsen said. "Why don't you walk with us? This is Joan Grieves, by the way. This is Father —"

"Monsignor," the old man said. "It is my only vanity. My family was very proud the day the cardinal made me a monsignor. Now my family is dead. Unfortunately, my vanity is not." He chuckled. "I sometimes believe that vanity is the last thing to die in a human being."

They set off to catch up with the events in front of the bank.

12:40 p.m.

Carney said, "You really think we need to do that?"

"I don't think we have any choice."

This was a reversal of their usual roles. Usually it was Carney proposing unnecessary violence and Petty objecting.

"I'll take the front," said Petty, "in case that's what's worrying you."

"You know better than that, Chief. No fear here." He grinned. He liked saying that to people. Especially when he was drunk. "Just — well, won't folks kind of think we're pushing too hard? Maybe we should give him a warning."

"We've given him a warning."

"Yeah, but we also killed his brother."

"You pulled the trigger."

"I'm just saying —"

Petty wondered if he might have a heart seizure. He had never felt this kind of pressure before. It had to be done and done quickly or anything could go wrong and it wouldn't be done at all. As he'd proposed to Carney . . . Carney would go around to the back door of the bank and wait for Petty to rush the bank, firing as he moved in. Carney would then smash the window in the back door and charge in that way. The cross fire was what Petty wanted. In the cross fire the bandit and Rattigan alike would be killed. And who could blame a good man like Petty who'd just been doing his job? He could argue that Rattigan was pretty much going to die anyway and that he was just making a last attempt to save him. Let some of the people bicker and question. He couldn't give a damn.

"You know he's going to kill Rattigan, anyway," said Petty.

"I can't argue with you there."

"So let's try and save him. We're the only hope Rattigan's got."

Carney nodded. "I keep forgetting he's a friend of yours."

"Yes," Petty said. "And I sure don't want to face Molly without telling her that I tried everything I could think of."

Carney sighed. "In case the bandit's watching, I'll kind of fade back into the crowd now. Then I'll take the long way around and come up on the back side of the bank."

"Good. I appreciate it."

Carney touched the back of his head. He was glad the rock hadn't hit him directly. The headache was mostly gone, but the goose egg was still sore as hell. "Well," he said, touching Petty on the sleeve. "Good luck to the both of us."

Petty was ready. In every crisis there was the best moment for action. He felt this situation had reached that moment. The robber was undoubtedly trapped in fear and rage — fear that he couldn't escape, rage that his brother had been killed. He wouldn't be thinking clearly. He'd be confused, uncertain.

Petty, on the other hand, knew just what he wanted to do and how to do it. He'd be firing into the front door as Carney was firing into the back door. The robber wouldn't know what to do. This was a death sentence for Rattigan.

Petty took out his railroad watch and checked it. He was just putting it away when he smelled his wife's perfume. Caroline was back.

She said, "I just saw Carney sneaking off. He's going to stir things up in there again, isn't he?"

"Caroline, do you have any idea the pressure I'm under right now? You know how my stomach gets so bad I can't eat? Well, it's even worse than that now. Won't you just go back there and stay with Molly? I'm doing the only thing I know how to do."

She said it then. She said it at great risk because if her assumption was wrong, then she would've revealed everything for nothing. "You know about Tom and me, don't you? That's why you're working to get him killed, isn't it?"

But his reaction let her know that he knew everything indeed. "You and Tom? You mean there's something going on between my faithful wife and my good friend Tom? I wish I had time to hear about all this, my faithful little wife. But right now, I don't. Maybe we can go over it tonight after the kids are in bed. Now, please, Caroline, get back there with Molly. Things are going to get kind of tense around here."

And it was just then that the bank door was flung open and Tom Rattigan appeared. He carried a large canvas money bag packed tight with greenbacks. The robber had his six-shooter pressed against Rattigan's head. "I want that horse and I want it right now."

He pushed Rattigan forward and then stepped out into the sunlight himself.

And that was when Petty grabbed Caroline and flung them both to the dusty street.

What happened next was what Petty had hoped would happen. His sudden movement had alarmed the already skittish outlaw. The robber interpreted this as a move against him. And then he did what he'd threatened to do. He shot Tom Rattigan.

Later, there would be various conflicting accounts of what happened. Some saw Rattigan try to jerk away from the arm the outlaw had around the banker's neck. Others saw Rattigan tromp hard on the outlaw's instep. And yet others saw Rattigan slam an elbow into the outlaw's ribs.

But even if all these things had happened — and none of them did — Rattigan wouldn't have escaped, anyway. Leonard had a firm hold on him. And he had the gun pressed tight to Rattigan's temple. Death was but a trigger pull away. And there could be no doubt that Rattigan was dead moments after Leonard fired. He died so quickly, in fact, that he couldn't get out an even halfway decent scream. His body flopped and flounced like a minstrel man doing a funny dance. And then the top of his head went flying away, and Leonard just let him drop to the street.

Leonard went into a crouch, firing bullet after bullet, frantically looking for some-place to hide. But there was no place. And so there — right in front of the law and all the townspeople — Walter Petty sent him down to his young and shabby death. Just some ignorant shitkicker who would prob-ably have been better off living his life in prison — dead now in the dusty street of a fairly unimportant town at the hands of a police chief who had pretty much manipu-lated everything since the luckless robbery began some three and a half hours earlier.

PART THREE

TWELVE

After it was all over, Monsignor Gomez told Father Madsen that Tom Rattigan's funeral was the largest ceremony ever held in the small, poor church. People came from as far away as four counties to the west. Rattigan may not have been beloved, the old prelate told Madsen, but he was respected because — despite his reputation for ruthlessness — he had actually helped many people in the area.

The monsignor found a cassock and surplice large enough for Madsen, who not only served as the main altar boy, but spent the two days between the killings and the funeral getting the church ready. The monsignor was too old and arthritic to do much. He gave rooms in the rectory to both Madsen and Joan. Joan found fresh flowers to decorate the altar, and spent a long day sweeping out the church and polishing up the battered wooden pews.

Madsen got the altar ready. He found High Mass vestments and altar dressings the monsignor had long forgotten he possessed. Then Madsen replaced all the nubs of altar candles with new ones. There were two stained-glass windows that had not been cleaned in some time. Madsen got a ladder, a bucket of soap and water, and set to work. The monsignor asked Madsen to choose the Bible readings. "There will be a lot of gringos here. I want to read something that will have meaning for them."

On the morning of the Funeral Mass, buggies, surreys, even a few hansoms formed a long line near the church. The funeral wagon was glass-encased and the pride of the Territory. A king would be happy to be taken to the cemetery in such a wagon. The driver even wore a top hat.

Between them, Madsen and Joan had managed to get the small pipe organ working again. The hot morning was filled with hymns played dramatically and well on the worn instrument. A chorus of young Mexican women sang sweetly, though the Spanish accent they brought to the Latin occasionally made Madsen smile.

Afterward, many people would tell the monsignor that the church had never looked so beautiful. The building gleamed and glistened and sparkled. The fresh flowers lent a sweetness that was almost narcotic. The mahogany casket was carried up the center aisle and placed before the communion rail by six pallbearers, good friends of Tom Rattigan's. The monsignor and Madsen were there to meet it. The monsignor immediately blessed it with holy water.

Molly Rattigan and her two children followed. The youngest girl wore a heavy veil. This would be the one with the port-wine stain, Madsen knew, the one who was ashamed of herself and who'd broken Rattigan's heart. Molly's pretty face was swollen from crying. Her other daughter had her arm around her mother's middle, as if supporting her. Molly touched the casket for a long moment before going into the pew. The chorus began a new hymn. The monsignor now blessed the casket with incense. The scent made the air even more glorious.

The mourners came next. All colors, shapes, ages, and, surprisingly, walks of life — rich and poor. Madsen assumed that the poor were those Rattigan was said to have helped.

Among the mourners were the Pettys. Walter wore a dark blue suit and a high collar and a blue cravat. He nodded to many of the mourners who were already seated. There was no particular expression on his face.

His wife, on the other hand, the truly beautiful Caroline, she looked as if she herself were about to be buried. Pale, frail, forlorn, she walked not with her husband but slightly behind him, her eyes fixed on some point in the distance. There was an ethereal quality to her blue gaze, one that might be a kind of divinity — or madness.

The Funeral Mass began. Elegant birds settled on the open windows to peer inside, the bell in the tower began to toll, and the music was so beautiful it made you forget for a moment why you were there.

Madsen renewed his faith. There was no other way to say it. For priests, like the faithful, Mass can become an ordeal, something to be dispatched as quickly and routinely as possible. He'd found himself guilty of this — if the priest isn't engaged in the holy rituals, what can you expect of the parishioners? — back at the mission. But he found himself reviewing his whole life as he knelt at the altar serving as the altar boy. His memories of Tom Rattigan were especially instructive to him. He'd always hated Tom — envied, feared him —

but he was glad he'd learned of Tom's love for his daughter and how Tom had helped at least a few of the needy of his town. Tom's soul hadn't been completely lost, anyway. Madsen just wished he'd spent some time with Tom. Tried to help him spiritually. And thinking this, Madsen realized again how kind God had been to him, to give Madsen a vocation in the priesthood after a life of wanton pleasuring, and then murder in the war.

He helped serve Walter Petty communion. He felt Petty's eyes on him as Petty drew near to the communion rail. Madsen's opinion was that the deaths of both Karl Schmitt and Tom Rattigan had been unnecessary. He'd mentioned this to several people, and he was sure that Petty had heard it by now.

Petty closed his eyes, put out his tongue.

The old monsignor held the host in trembling fingers and set it on Petty's tongue. Then it was on to the next communicant.

The burial itself was on the side of a slope near a line of jack pines. It was too hot and too dry, and several of the horses got skittish when a nearby train roared by. And the monsignor got confused at several points in the ritual, and finally turned it all over to Madsen. The monsignor had not said a High Mass in a long time, and the experience had worn him out.

A long luncheon followed the graveyard services. Madsen was amused to see that Joan and the monsignor sat together at a small table. In just two days, she had righted his priestly affairs. Correspondence dating back as far as a year she'd cleared up, and his den was set in order. She didn't stop there. She washed and scrubbed the monsignor's bedroom, aired it out. She washed and pressed his shabby cassocks. And she began making him three good meals a day. Madsen sensed all this was very good for her. If she didn't seem happy exactly, at least for a time, she seemed able to escape the gloom over her father and her oddly mixed feelings about Rattigan's death.

Madsen himself was much in demand. Flirting with a handsome priest was a pastime for many churchwomen. Completely safe and yet thrilling at the same time. He enjoyed it, too. What man wouldn't? While he was celibate, he wasn't dead. A pretty lady was still a pretty lady.

He ate, drank a little more wine than was perhaps advisable, and joined the others in letting the afternoon drift away, the shadows on the mountains purple now, the air itself melancholy with the dying day. The bark of dogs always sounded lonely at this time, and mothers began calling their children in. Joan had taken the monsignor back to the rectory three hours ago.

The long outdoor tables at which the guests had sat were mostly empty now. He was just rolling himself a cigarette when he looked up and saw Caroline Petty standing there. She was still pale, still had the look of somebody who'd just seen something terrible, yet could not pull herself away from it.

"Everybody's very pleased, the way you pitched in for the funeral," she said. "People think highly of you."

"Thanks. But it really wasn't all that much."

"I should tell you, I'm not a Catholic."

He smiled. "Well, I've been known to talk to a few non-Catholics in my time."

"That's what I wanted, Father. A time to talk to you. I —" She hesitated. "About Tom. I know you grew up with him."

"I should tell you that we weren't necessarily friends."

"That's the funny thing. When he talked about you, he always said he liked you very much but that he knew you disapproved of him."

"I'm afraid I did."

She paused. "I'd still like to talk to you. I was wondering about tonight."

"After dinner sometime?"

"Eight-thirty. Get the kids to bed."

"That'd be fine."

He said, "Your husband's behind that pillar over there. Watching us talk. I get the impression he doesn't like seeing you talk to me."

"Right now I don't give a damn what he likes, Father. If you'll forgive me swearing."

"He just left."

"Eight-thirty o'clock, then. And thank you very much."

He walked back to the rectory. He wanted to walk off the wine. He had a fondness for the grape, and sometimes that troubled him. The same way staring at pretty women too long sometimes troubled him. But as an old priest he'd known in the seminary always said, "Without temptation, there could be no virtue."

Joan was in total charge of the rectory. He came in the back door of the small adobe house and she said, "Please take your boots off, Father. I scrubbed the floors today and I don't want all the red dust tracked everywhere."

He smiled. "Yes, Commander."

She laughed. "I do sound kind of bossy, don't I?"

"A little. But it's sort of sweet."

"Sweet and bossy. Now that's a nice combination for a girl. But I was serious about the boots. Please take them off."

She fed him. The monsignor was asleep, worn out. When the meal was done, he rolled them each a cigarette. Every once in a while, she liked to indulge.

"I like it here," she said.

"So I gather."

"You mind that?"

"Why would I mind?"

"Well, I never pitched in back at the mission the way I have here."

"I've never needed the help the monsignor does. Plus, you've changed. You obviously feel more of a need to help. And that's good for you. Gets you out of yourself. Sometimes I think that's the worst trap of all — ourselves. It's so hard to get away from all our own thoughts and problems and complications. That's the nice part about helping others. It makes you concentrate on them."

She exhaled a long graceful arc of blue-white smoke. "You change tobaccos?"

"Yeah."

"This is nice."

"It's really pipe tobacco."

"It's sweeter."

Then: "I'm going to have company in a while. Caroline Petty," Father Madsen said.

"She's beautiful."

"She certainly is that."

"Her husband's back in favor, I guess."

"Oh?"

"The first couple days, a lot of people around the church were mad at the way Petty handled everything. Getting Rattigan and the robbers killed. Now they seem to be coming around to the way he explained things. That even more people would've been killed if he hadn't pushed it with that robber."

"People don't like to concentrate on bad things. It's easier to just go along with the easiest explanation and get on with their lives."

"You still think he forced a showdown?"

"Don't you?"

She exhaled another elegant plume of smoke. "Yeah; yeah, I guess I do. And I still can't figure out why."

She cleaned up the dinner table, and then went in and worked for a time on the study where he'd meet Caroline Petty. Her energy and purpose amazed him. Made him feel old. He couldn't find that energy inside him and he knew it.

He read the local newspaper and smoked his pipe. Joan was right. The newspaper editorial was about how Petty had handled the bank robbery. "While some may disagree with the police chief's desire to force a rapid conclusion, this editor would like to remind folks of three other similar hostage situations which turned into bloodbaths because law enforcement officials didn't act soon enough." The editorial then went on to list some recent examples. Madsen didn't find this surprising. You might second-guess a police chief with a dubious record, but from what Madsen had heard about Petty, he was an intelligent, honest, and effective lawman. In most circumstances, he would deserve the support of his community at a time like this. But still, there was something unspoken that bothered Madsen about this. . . .

Caroline put the girls to bed early. They complained vociferously — and she did feel a little guilty — but she read them a couple of stories and that seemed to settle them in.

She went downstairs. The desert night being chilly, she grabbed her light cape. The hood was dusty, and she brushed it off.

Walter was in his study. He had a drink of whiskey and a cigar. He was looking through some of the many reports he had to file these days. As someone had said recently, policemen no longer carried guns, they carried forms to fill out. That was only half a joke.

"I thought I'd go over to Milly's," she said from the doorway.

"Good old Milly." He thought a moment. "Say, I thought you didn't like good old Milly."

"Well, we had that silly argument about that schoolteacher she didn't like. But we got over it."

His gaze went cold. "You're usually pretty good at getting over things, aren't you, Caroline?"

The implication wasn't exact. But then it didn't need to be.

"I won't be long," she said.

As she started to turn and leave, he said, "You said something to me during the robbery about Tom. That I knew something about you two." He set the papers down and looked hard at her. "You never said

that and I never heard it. Do you understand?"

"You're asking me to lie?"

"To lie? No, my dear. I'm asking you to
consider your reputation. And I'm also
asking you to consider what might happen
to our girls if word ever got around that —
well, let's just say that their mother left
certain things to be desired in her moral
conduct. That's a nice way to say it, don't
you think? Moral conduct?"

"Does that mean you'd tell them?"

The iciness left his tone. He seemed genuinely surprised by her words. "God, you
can really surprise me sometimes, Caroline. I always think of you as so intelligent
and then you say something like that." He
sighed deeply. "Do you think I want to destroy our family? Or do you think I want to
be known as a cuckold? What kind of police chief would I be if I was involved in a
scandal like that? And can you imagine
what our girls would go through at school
if the other children started taunting
them?" He paused. "You didn't think a
damn thing about what you were doing,
did you?"

"No, I suppose I didn't."

"Well, you'd better start thinking things
through now before it's too late. Think of

the girls — and me."

She slumped against the doorway. "You still want me as a wife?"

"Is that such a terrible fate? Being my wife?" The iciness was in his voice again.

"I loved him. I still do."

He stood up and came to her. Put his large hands on her small shoulders. "That's something else you didn't say and something else I didn't hear."

She tried to push away from his embrace, but he wouldn't let her.

"You killed him, Walt."

"No, I didn't. Leonard Schmitt killed him. You saw it yourself."

"You killed his brother to set this all in motion."

"You're wrong again, Caroline. Red Carney killed him. Ask him. He'll tell you."

"Because you'd turn him over on that stagecoach-money charge if he hadn't."

She pushed against him. He let her go.

"You didn't read the editorial yet, I guess," he said. "About how I don't deserve to be second-guessed by people in this town. About how I've been a good police chief — and I don't think even you'd deny that — and about how I just might have saved a lot of lives by doing what I did."

"You killed Tom Rattigan because you knew we were lovers."

His slap was swift and powerful. Her head cracked back against the door frame. "I don't want to ever hear you say that again."

"It's the truth," she said, touching the back of her head where the pain was worst. "It's the truth and there's nothing you can do to change it."

He grabbed her wrist. "Well, if you like the truth so much, why don't you go upstairs and wake the girls up and tell them everything that happened? How you put his cock in your mouth and he fucked you on the floor of the gazebo."

"You watched us!"

"As much as I could stand, I watched. And then I went in the woods and threw up. And then you know what? I cried. I cried because the mother of my daughters is a whore. I cried because the woman I've given my entire life to is a slut. You make it sound like I took some pleasure in watching you. Believe me, I didn't. I just wanted to make sure that I wasn't having some jealous fantasy again. But unfortunately, I wasn't. Unfortunately, my wife was just the pig I suspected she was."

This time his slap was so strong it

knocked her into the wall across from the door. She slid down to the floor and began weeping.

"There now," he said. "I've said my piece and we never have to have this conversation again now, do we, Caroline? Think of the girls, Caroline. They're the most important things in our life. If you started telling people that I pushed Leonard Schmitt into killing Tom — think of what that would do to the girls." He looked down at her with great sadness. "Or don't you think you've done enough to this family already?"

THIRTEEN

Carney had never been a hero before. Not in reality. Like most men, he'd had daydreams of derring-do and all the appropriate rewards that went with derring-do. In the old red schoolhouse he'd saved several pretty little girls over and over again from villains of various kinds, most of which resembled the villains in the dime novels he read. But as for being a real hero . . .

The thing was, in these circumstances at least, he didn't quite enjoy it. Men who'd always sniggered about him and his drinking problem now stepped up to shake his hand and clap his back and talk about what a fine job of shooting he'd done the other day, picking off that Karl Schmitt the way he had. And they wanted to assure him that Chief Petty had damned well done the right thing, too, pressing the issue, that's the only way you could deal with scum like the Schmitts, press the damned issue and then kill the bastards on the spot.

He sat in the back of the police station drinking coffee. It was ten a.m. He should be out on the street.

Walt Petty came in.

"Hey," Petty said, carrying his cup of coffee over and sitting down at the same small table as Carney. "There's the hero of the hour. The way people are talking around here, you could be the next mayor."

His voice sounded strained and loud in the silence. "You all right, Red?"

Carney shrugged. "I'm fine."

"You don't sound fine."

He looked up at Petty. His eyes were bloodshot. But this time it was from lack of sleep, not whiskey. He glanced at the doorway, then leaned forward to speak in a stage whisper. "The thing is, Chief, it bothers me."

"What bothers you? Having people admire you after all these years of treating you like a joke? Giving your wife and kids a reason to be proud of you instead of ashamed? Being a credit to this department for once instead of a liability? Are those the things that bother you, Red? Because if they are, then I'd have to say you don't show much gratitude for the opportunity that got dropped in your lap."

"Opportunity?" Carney said, sounding shocked. "You think killing a man in cold blood is an opportunity?"

"He would have killed other people in there."

"No, he wouldn't. You heard what the hostages said. The one I killed had to turn his gun over to his brother because he *wouldn't* kill people."

"Well, now, just how the hell were we supposed to know that, Red? We had to play the hand we were dealt."

Carney put his head down. This time when he spoke, he could barely be heard. "I just don't know why you wanted to get Tom Rattigan killed."

"Now where would you get an idea like that?"

"You said yourself —"

"Red . . ." Calmly, patiently, almost as if he were talking to a child. "Red, I remember my words exactly. I said, 'If that's how things turn out, that's how they turn out.'"

"But I told you you were gonna get him killed. And you *knew* he was gonna be killed."

"I did? Now be sensible, Red. How

could I *know* he was going to be killed? I was handling that hostage situation the best way I could. You go around telling people stories like that, they're liable to think you're drinking again. And you know what? You go around telling stories like that and people aren't going to think you're a hero anymore, either. They're going to think you don't have what it takes to be a hero. You had to kill a man in order to save a lot of other lives and you couldn't even do that without whining. They're sure not going to think much of you, Red. And neither are your wife and kids. And neither am I. In fact, that kind of talk, I wouldn't even want you on the force anymore, Red. It wouldn't be good for morale, you going around like that. It really wouldn't."

Just then the Mexican man who swept the place came back and said, "I clean now, Chief?"

"Sure, Paco. I was just leaving." He stood up. "This is quite a man we have here, isn't he, Paco?"

"*Sí*," Paco said. "People say he is the best man with a rifle in the whole Territory. They talk much about him. Much. All the little children, they have their sticks for guns. They all say they are Red Carney,

Bang-bang. 'I am Red Carney, *Señor.*' They are very much fun, the little children."

"I guess you heard that for yourself now, didn't you, Red?" Petty said, and strode out of the back room.

Carney sat there thinking about a drink. He'd awakened in the middle of the night with the tremors. He'd had a dream about the man he'd killed. He knew some men, they actually liked killing other men. There was real pleasure for them in it. In his first days on the force, he hadn't believed them, attributed their boasting to them just being men. Men liked to talk hard that way, as much to impress themselves as others. Maybe if they talked loud enough and long enough, they could convince themselves that they were really as fierce as they liked to claim. There was something almost superstitious about it. It was good luck to talk hard because when the time came to *be* hard, maybe you could actually be as tough as you needed to be. But over the years he'd come to know men who weren't just bragging at all. They *enjoyed* killing. Now he wished he was one of them. If it had been in self-defense, killing Karl Schmitt, that would've been one thing. But to kill him without warning — and to kill him just so that would set in motion Tom Rattigan's death . . . Any way you looked at it, Petty had to know that Rattigan was the number one hostage and would be killed in any kind of confrontation. It was killing by proxy, just one step removed from Petty asking Carney to shoot Tom Rattigan directly.

He finished up his coffee. Damn, he wanted a drink.

Caroline was in the garden when the priest came. She felt good seeing him there, as if someone had thrown her a lifeline. She liked the combination of masculine strength and gentleness she sensed in him. In his work shirt and jeans, you'd never know he was a priest. She'd been tending her seasonal flowers — the ones that would grow in this part of the country, anyway — when he stepped into sight and said, "I'm glad to see you're all right."

She stood up. "I'm sorry I didn't get to the rectory last night. My husband and I had a talk and — well, I decided it'd be best if I didn't talk to you."

"I just wanted to make sure nothing had happened to you."

She flushed. "I'm sorry if I gave you the impression there was any kind of serious trouble. I — the talk with my husband was what I needed."

He said, "You knew Tom Rattigan."

"Why, yes, I did. He was one of my husband's best friends."

"The way you looked at the funeral yesterday. I just wondered — his death must have affected you pretty deeply."

"Well, yes — and for Molly, too. Molly's my best friend."

"I see."

He wouldn't take his eyes from her. They remained a challenge to the untruths she was telling.

"The way your husband pushed everything to a showdown at the bank — it almost seemed as if he wanted Rattigan killed."

"You have no right to say that," she snapped. But her anger only betrayed her. Her anger only revealed that she recognized the truth of his words and was frightened by it. "My husband is a good man."

The accusatory look was replaced by a gentler one. "I'm trying to help you, Caroline. I think I know what happened. After you've heard confessions for a lot of years — we're all weak, Caroline. We're all sinners. Sometimes when somebody's troubled in a marriage — they turn to other people. Sometimes they don't even plan to, it just works out that way. It's wrong in the strictest sense, but I try never to judge people for it. Loneliness and disappointment can make people do a lot of things they wouldn't ordinarily do. Tom could be a very charming man. Even when we were kids, he was the one all the girls got a crush on." He smiled. "I remember him stealing a girlfriend or two of mine."

She surprised him — and herself — by returning his smile. A nostalgic one. "He was like that as a kid?"

"Very much. We lived in an orphanage. The kids at school didn't like us much. They made fun of us — Tom and a man named Noah Grieves and me. We each had our own ways of making ourselves feel better. Noah kept his head stuck in a book. I tended to use my fists way too much. And Tom made himself feel better by getting girls to fall in love with him. I guess it proved to him that he was worth knowing — you know, something more than a scrubby kid from the orphanage."

She said it then — despite her instincts, which said no, despite anything remotely resembling her better judgement. "I loved him, Father. I never was in love ever before. When I married Walt — he'd saved the lives of my parents. I respected him and was grateful to him and knew that he would be a good husband, but I wasn't in love with him. I'm not even sure I loved him in the way you love a friend. He's cold and calculating. I don't think he even means to be. That's just his nature."

The tears came, then. Soft tears, shamed tears. "I caused his death. If I'd broken it off the way I should've — he'd be alive today."

"I'm not sure what you mean."

If Walt hadn't seen us together in the gazebo, he'd never have known what was going on. If I'd ended that affair like a good and decent woman three or four months earlier — and concentrated on my children the way I should've — then we wouldn't have been there that night and Walt wouldn't have seen us. And Tom would be alive today.

But she couldn't say this, of course. What Walt had said made sense. If she told people what she knew — how Walt had contrived the standoff so that Tom would almost certainly be killed — the girls would suffer. They would be shamed the rest of their lives. Look what their mother had done. Look what their father had done. Their lives would be changed forever.

"I can't talk about it, Father. I really can't. You guessed about Tom and me — I shouldn't even have told you it happened. I guess it's guilt. I guess I just needed to admit it to somebody. But as far as Walt goes — he didn't kill Tom. He really didn't." *Leonard Schmitt killed Tom. Now how was that my fault? If you told people Walt killed him, they'd just look at you. Everybody saw it, they'd say. Leonard Schmitt killed poor Tom Rattigan. Not Walt.* She could hear Walt saying this to her. He was a very confident man, her husband.

Mom hadn't believed Celia.

At breakfast this morning, Celia had said, "I saw Daddy last night."

"You mean you dreamed about him, sweetheart?"

"No, I saw him."

Her older sister Ellie and her mother looked at each other. "I see."

"He was standing at the end of my bed. In the middle of the night. It was funny. He was there, but at the same time I could see right through him."

"Oh, honey," Mom said gently. "You were dreaming."

"He said he loved us all and would see us again someday." Then: "And he said something else, too." She hesitated. "He said what you said last night to Uncle Roger. About Chief Petty."

Mom frowned. "You were supposed to be in bed asleep."

"I just got up to get a drink. And then I heard voices downstairs. So I just sat on the stairs and listened."

"That was between your uncle Roger and me. Adults. Not little girls."

"I'm ten. That's not so little."

"For talk like that it is."

"Do you really think that Chief Petty made it so that Daddy had to get killed?"

Mom flushed. "I don't want to discuss this with you. I told you, it's for adults."

"I'll bet you discussed it with Ellie."

"Ellie's older."

"Just twelve."

Mom's gaze turned sad. "I'm sorry, sweetheart. You were his special love. I keep forgetting that." She leaned over and took her daughter's slender hand. "He loved you with all his heart."

"I just want to know about Chief Petty."

"I'm more interested in what you saw last night," Molly said, glancing at Ellie.

"Maybe it was a ghost," Ellie offered tentatively.

"Mom doesn't believe in ghosts," Celia

said. "And neither do you."

"Who said I don't believe in ghosts?" Ellie said.

"You. I asked you about ghosts once and you said ghosts were just for little kids."

"Well, maybe I changed my mind."

"You changed your mind because you and Mom don't want to talk about Chief Petty."

"I shouldn't have said anything about the man," Mom said. "I was just feeling angry was all. I suppose he did what he needed to do."

"But you said it and so did Uncle Roger."

"Well, if you really want to know —" And for the first time since his death Molly's face displayed a quick, small smile. "We were drunk."

"Mother!" Ellie, who was very conscious of being proper, said. "And in front of Celia."

"Well, it's true," Mom said. "I was drunk. And so was your uncle Roger." Then the frivolity of the moment left her face. "I'm trying to be strong and brave for you girls, but inside I'm very goddamn angry. And don't tell me that I'm taking the Lord's name in vain because I know I am. But under the circumstances — me losing my husband and you losing your father — I think the Lord will understand my language. And maybe even forgive me."

That was the note breakfast had concluded on. Now Celia was back in her room. On her bed. Reading a magazine for girls. It was funny. She could be reading along and then she'd just break into tears. No warning. And no restraint. Just sob . . .

And downstairs, in Tom's den, it was no better with Molly. She sat at his desk, holding his Civil War pistol in her hand. There were bullets for it in the drawer. She was sure it would fire. If the target was close enough . . . That sonofabitch found out what was going on and figured out a way of killing him and getting away with it. If only he'd realized that these affairs meant nothing to Tom. Caroline would be Petty's again in just a few weeks, maybe even sooner. Tom would have been thoroughly done with her. But, no, he had to kill him. Maybe it wouldn't matter if he'd *known* Tom would give her back. Maybe it was that damned strutting male pride of Walter's. Maybe it didn't matter. Maybe he just wanted Tom dead for having slept with Caroline.

She held the gun in her hand, stroking the barrel gently, the way she'd once stroked Tom. Caroline would have gone back to Walter and Tom would have come back to Molly. That was just the way things had been, and she'd learned long ago that if she wanted Tom to stay around, those were his terms. As long as other people in town didn't know. As long as the girls didn't know. As long as her mother didn't know . . . A smile again. Her mother didn't believe in letting men push women around. She would have been enraged if she'd known about Tom. . . .

For the first time as she sat there, she began wondering seriously about the bullets for the gun. Were they in fact in the drawer? Would the gun in fact still fire? It was an idle fantasy to be sure, but . . .

She opened the first drawer on the left. Not there. The second drawer. Not there, either. Nor the third. Nor the first or second on the right. But there in the third drawer . . . there was a box of cartridges.

She could imagine Walter's face when she walked up to him and shot him. He would die in shock and disbelief. Mild Molly Rattigan shooting somebody? You wouldn't think a woman like that would even know how to fire a gun. (He didn't know about all the lessons her older brothers had given her.) And so, with his face a mixture of pain and complete astonishment, he would die there on the street just as poor Tom had.

She took out the box of bullets. Old, dusty. Would the bullets even be any good after all this time?

Then she started loading the gun. It felt good. All the sorrow of the past few days . . . She knew she wouldn't actually go through with it — mild Molly Rattigan? — but it felt good nonetheless to *think* about it, to *plan* it as if it were really going to happen. . . .

Yes, indeed, it felt so good.

And then, without her quite realizing it, the gun was loaded. And now it was a very different object in her hand. No longer just an empty-chambered memento. Oh, no, this gun had heft and *purpose*. Mild Molly Rattigan . . . too bad she wouldn't ever have the nerve to use it. Because Walter Petty had killed her husband and she had no doubt about that whatsoever.

Joan went looking for Father Madsen, and found him in the front pew of the church. Street clothes. Just sitting by himself. She went over and sat next to him.

"You were up and down a lot last night, Father."

"Did I wake you up?"

"No, I wasn't sleeping too well myself." She glanced at the altar. It had a majesty for her; she had such good memories of growing up at the mission and Father Madsen there saying Mass. Now that things had been resolved to some degree, she found herself thinking of children again. She wanted three or four. She would bring them to church each Sunday in gingham bonnets and dresses. Their father, who would be a big and handsome man like this priest, he would be proud to be in such fine company as his wife and children. They would be respectable people and others would be happy to be their friends. She wanted to be respectable; she had not been so for a long time, since Rattigan had framed her father. She did not want power or wealth. Just to be an average person people did not smirk at when she walked down the street, someone boys weren't afraid to court because her father was in Yuma prison.

"Why weren't *you* sleeping well?" Father Madsen asked.

"Same reason you weren't, probably. Tom Rattigan. Whatever I thought of him, he didn't deserve to die that way."

"You were going to kill him yourself."

"I was wrong. I can see that now. I detest what he did to my father, but Petty really bothers me. At least, if I would've killed him, I would've been punished. Prison or maybe even the gallows. But he's got a badge, so he's going to get away with it."

"I've been thinking about Carney."

"What about him?"

"He's the only one who knows for sure what Petty was thinking. He's the one who killed Karl Schmitt through the bank window. And he didn't want to do it. I could see that when I was up there on the roof. He knew he was committing murder. But he said that Petty had ordered him to, or else he'd fire him."

They sat in silence for a time. The sunlight through the stained-glass windows glazed the wooden floor with golden-yellow and wine-red and sky-blue and forest-green, so vividly that the wooden floor seemed to be covered with a brilliant carpet. A young dog wandered in — he was a frequent visitor — and Father Madsen got up, walked over to him, petted him several times, and then led him outside.

Father Madsen sat down next to Joan

again and said, "He's thinking of con-
verting."

She laughed. "The dog?"

"Uh-huh."

"Well, what religion is he now?"

"Lutheran. He wants to be an altar boy."

She laughed again.

Then they were silent once again.

"I guess I'll go see him," said Madsen.

"I thought you might."

"It's asking a lot of him."

"Everybody tells me he's a very decent
man," she said, "except when he's drinking."

"Thank God I was spared that particular demon. I drink too much as it is. But
being a drunkard —" He just shook his
head.

"You know I'm staying here, don't you?"

"I thought you might."

"Monsignor Gomez needs me, and
there are a lot more young men in this
town."

He leaned over and kissed her tenderly
on the mouth. "I'm going to miss you."

"You never kissed me like that before."

"I've wanted to for a long time."

She took his hand. "I'll always love you
and think about you, Father." Then, after a
time of just looking at each other, she said,

"I hope Carney decides to help you."

"So do I," he said.

A few minutes later, he went looking for the man.

The first place Madsen went was the police station. Logical enough. That was where Carney, now reinstated as an assistant police chief, generally spent his mornings.

He was about ten feet from the boardwalk in front of the station when a uniformed patrolman came out.

"Morning," Madsen said.

"Morning," the cop said, seeming affable enough.

"Would Assistant Chief Carney happen to be in there?"

"Afraid not. He had some appointments this morning."

"Oh, well, thank you."

Madsen walked away. The front door of the station opened and Petty walked out. He'd been in the front part of the station and seen Madsen through the window.

Petty called for the cop to come back. "I saw you talking to that man Madsen."

"Oh, is that his name, Chief? I didn't know who he was."

"What did he want?"

"He was looking for Carney."

"Carney? Why the hell did he want Carney?"

The cop shrugged. "I don't know, sir. He didn't say. Is that all, sir?"

"Yes," Petty said. "Thanks."

"Sure," the cop said, leaving now on his morning rounds.

Carney, Petty wondered as he stood there. *There's only one reason he could be looking for Carney. What the hell did those two talk about when they were up on that roof? Carney had a very loose tongue when he was drinking, and he'd been drinking that morning. Had he told the priest anything the priest could use? Carney would, of course, present himself as the complete innocent pushed around by the big bad chief. The trouble was, despite his well-deserved reputation as a drunkard, some people took Carney seriously. If he ever started mouthing off about Petty . . . but then would he be that foolish? He was the one who'd pulled the trigger. If there were ever to be questions about why Karl Schmitt had been killed in the manner he had, Carney would be judged just as guilty as Petty. That was the trouble with somebody as prominent as Tom Rattigan getting killed . . . too many important Rattigan friends not really satisfied with how things had been handled; important people who became dangerous*

282

people with all their questions and doubts. Dangerous people who weren't afraid to challenge Petty.

He went back inside. He was not a happy man.

FOURTEEN

"Maybe you shouldn't be doing this, Red."

"I didn't ask for a sermon. I just want a drink."

"It ain't even eleven yet."

"I know how to tell the time."

"And you just got back in Petty's good graces."

"Yeah, and you know *how* I got in his good graces?"

"You killed a man."

"Yeah, in cold blood."

Jennings was used to lawmen in his saloon. It was their preferred hangout. Some were tougher than others. There was a popular notion that killing a man didn't bother most lawmen. That was wrong. Some it didn't; others, like Carney here, it had the power to destroy. Some men just weren't killers. For all his Irish rage and brawling, Jennings had never killed a man, and wasn't inclined to think he'd like it.

Jennings said kindly, "He was a bank robber, Red."

"But he hadn't killed anybody. And that's the point."

"But maybe he would've."

"Maybe. But we don't know that for sure, and I guess that's what bothers me so much."

"Most folks think Petty did the right thing."

Carney thought again of the conversation he'd had with Petty right before going up on the roof. "Yeah, I guess Petty would think he did the right thing. He's got that kind of pride."

Jennings leaned forward again. "You better not let him hear you talking this way. He sure wouldn't like it."

Carney said, "Just give me a beer then."

"Beer's a drink, too, Red. I better not. You just got back on your feet. Think of your wife and kids."

"Hell, Jennings, then I'll just go somewhere else. I need a drink and there's nothin' I can do about it."

Jennings sighed. "I sure don't want to do this, Red. I sure don't."

He served him a beer.

Ellie came home for lunch. She went to

a private school where the girls had much more freedom than they would have in the public school.

She called for her mother, but couldn't find her. She asked the maid, and the maid pointed to the study. "I'm kinda worried about her, Miss Ellie."

"Why?"

"You'll see."

Ellie did not like enigmatic remarks from the help. She considered them impertinent. But before she could ask the maid to explain, the maid managed to slip away.

Ellie went down the hall. The study door was slightly ajar. She peeked in. She eased the door open with a single finger and peeked inside.

Her mother Molly sat at her father's desk. Stared out the window. Seemed completely lost in whatever thoughts she was having. Nothing wrong with this. Death made most people introspective.

The trouble was the gun she held in her hand. The trouble was the box of bullets on the desktop. The trouble was Mom knew a lot about guns and could use one competently.

"Mom."

"Oh, hi."

"Our maid — who speaks in riddles —

seems to be worried about you."

"Worried about me? Honey, I'm just going through the normal things a wife does when she loses a husband."

"I hate to say it, but I think our enigmatic maid may have a point."

"Oh?"

"Mom, maybe you're not aware of it, but you seem to be holding a gun in your hand. Father's Civil War pistol."

"I'm just holding it, Ellie. That's all. What's the harm in that?"

"That box of bullets — did you load the gun?"

"Yes, I did, darling. Now are there any more questions?"

"Yes, Mother," Ellie said in her best private-school-sophisticated tone. "What are you planning to do with the gun?"

Molly's face showed irritation. "I really don't like your tone. Or all your questions. Don't I have a right to take your father's gun down by the creek and do a little target practice?"

"For what reason?"

"My God, Ellie, because I *feel* like it. Isn't *that* a good enough reason? Because my father and your father and I used to do target practice together all the time. And because I have good memories of those days. And because right now that's all I have to hold on to — memories, Ellie. Because I'm not a young, beautiful woman like you with her whole life ahead of her. I've spent my life with your father, and right now I need to cling to his memory any way I can. So I'm taking his *damned* pistol down to the *damned* creek and doing some *damned* shooting. If that is all right with you, I mean."

But Ellie wasn't intimidated by her mother's scorn. "I just don't want you getting any queer ideas."

"Queer ideas? Now tell me, dear daughter, exactly what would a queer idea be?"

"Getting back at Walter Petty."

"I see."

"I know you blame him for Father's death. So do I. Father would probably be alive today if it wasn't for Petty. But that still doesn't mean one of us should pick up a gun and —"

Ellie was surprised by her mother's answer. She'd expected Mother to brush away Ellie's suspicion. Instead, Mother said, "So he just gets away with it? I know something you don't. And I know that he arranged everything to ensure that your father would be killed. And so we just forget about it? We just let him go on with his life and enjoy himself — while you're without a father and I'm without a husband?"

"Oh, God, Mother," Ellie said, all her sophistication gone, just a scared young daughter now rushing to her mother and kneeling next to her and pressing her mother's free hand to her face. "Oh, please say you won't do anything, Mother. You're terrifying me. You really are."

Her mother set the gun down. Stared at it. "I still remember him in his uniform. He was so handsome. He hadn't been much of a shot until my father took him in hand. Daddy even offered to buy his way out of the war, but Tom said no. It was his duty. I don't think I got a single good night's sleep the whole time he was gone." Then she surprised her daughter by looking at her and smiling. "I'm not going to do anything crazy, honey. I'm really not."

Caroline had spent most of the night sitting in the girls' room by the moon-glowing window. Sitting. Thinking. Praying. She had decided that Walt was right. Anything she did now, she would only destroy the girls. And she couldn't do that. Even if she asked for a divorce, her affair with

Tom Rattigan would become public knowledge. She would look like a bitter wife if she offered the conjecture that Walt had masterminded his murder.

She was tired now as she sat across from Walt in the kitchen where he was eating his lunch.

She said, "I wanted to let you know that I'm going to do what you want."

He looked up from his soup. "Meaning what exactly?"

"Meaning I'll be your wife."

"In name only?"

She hesitated. "I'm not sure yet."

"I am." He put his spoon next to his soup. "I want you to be my wife again. My real wife. You can't love a dead man."

"This isn't about Tom. It's about you."

"Me? I didn't have the affair."

"But you had him killed."

He picked up his spoon. Ate some of his vegetable soup. "I thought you weren't going to say that anymore."

"I just want you to know where I stand. I might've gotten over Tom. As much as I was taken with him, I was certainly aware of his faults. But what you did — that's something I'll never get over. Knowing you were capable of it."

"I saw the mayor this morning. He says

the governor's going to give me a citation."

"Won't that be wonderful." Her sarcasm was searing. "I don't want it in the house."

"A citation from the governor? I want it in my study."

"It really doesn't bother you, does it."

"I was doing my job."

"Settling scores is what you were doing."

"If it bothers you that much, I'll keep the citation at the office."

"I appreciate that."

"See, there's no reason we can't be husband and wife again. We just need to talk things through."

"That simple, is it?"

He finished his soup. "That simple if you want it to be." He said, "I'd like to make love soon. I'm a normal, healthy man with normal, healthy needs."

"I don't know if I can. Not right away anyway."

"I might have to insist. Dr. Robert says I'm developing prostate trouble, that I need to keep that sac empty as much as possible."

"How romantic."

He fixed her with an eye that was surprisingly loving. "I'd be happy to be romantic again if you'd let me."

"I don't want you to be romantic. Ever."

He put down his linen napkin. "All this will take some time. I'm well aware of that. You need to do some adjusting and *I* need to do some adjusting. I hate to remind you, but I'm the wronged party here. Not you. Not Tom."

"Tom isn't the wronged party? You killed him."

"You keep saying that. Carney killed him." He added, "You haven't touched your soup."

"This isn't going to work," she said miserably. "I can't go through with this charade."

"It doesn't have to be a charade." Then: "And think of the girls. Do you want to tell them that we're divorcing? Do you want them to find out in court what their mother's been up to?"

"How about what their *father's* been up to."

He waved his hand. "Again, vague accusations. And nothing will come of them. Nothing."

"If Carney told the truth, they would."

"Carney." He shook his head. "Carney is a very sad man who's clinging to his job. If he *did* say anything, I'd fire him. And then what? He'd been a drunken ex-policeman who has a grudge against me.

Who'd believe him?"

"Other people have doubts about what happened. They might believe him."

"Every time a lawman fires his gun, somebody has doubts. Judges and juries know all about the doubts, and they still only convict lawmen very rarely. Lawmen, whether you like them or not, are the average citizen's only line of defense. Most people remember that. You grew up in a very rarefied home, Caroline. You had servants and bodyguards. You didn't need lawmen. At least not directly. But you can bet that every time your father needed something not quite legal done, he'd get ahold of his favorite lawman and ask him to do it. Your father's a wealthy man, and wealthy men look at lawmen as their indentured slaves. It's a terrible thing to say, but it's the truth — in both senses. That's how rich men look at us — and that's how we act around them. Yes, sir, no, sir, whatever you say, sir. It makes me sick, but it happens. *I've* even had to do it from time to time. The average person doesn't have that kind of privilege, so he's much more willing to give us the benefit of the doubt because he knows *he* sure doesn't want to go out there and face all the bad people we do."

"That's a nice little speech."

"It's true."

"You don't have much faith in the common man."

He smiled. "Caroline, please don't waste your time trying to tell me that you know anything about the common man. Because you don't."

"I know they want the truth. I know they want their lawmen to live by the same rules they have to. I know that a lot of the common men around here liked Tom Rattigan because he helped them."

"He helped them because he wanted to be governor someday. He was an arrogant peacock and you know it."

He stood up. Walked over to her. Tried to kiss her. But she turned her face away.

"This will only work if you *let* it work, Caroline. What happens when the girls see us like this? Father can't even give Mother a little peck on the cheek? You don't think they'll wonder what's going on? You don't think this'll upset them? Now, let me give you a little peck on the cheek. I'm not asking you to take your clothes off. Just a simple, civil kiss. That's your end of this bargain, Caroline, and if you can't handle it you'd better say so now. Because if that's the case, then I want you to tell the girls tonight that we're divorcing." He paused. "Can you picture their faces? Can you imagine the terrible pain in their eyes? Can you imagine what this will do to them when they try and play around their friends? Because everybody will be talking about it, Caroline. People are interested in us. People love scandals, and believe me, we'll be quite the scandal. 'Chief Petty? Did you hear about his wife having an adulterous affair? The poor man.' That's what the girls will hear, too. For years and years they'll hear that. And they'll carry it with them the rest of their lives. Is that what you want, Caroline? Think it over this afternoon, and then make up your mind by tonight. Because if you're not going to be my wife — my *real* wife — then I want to start the divorce immediately. And I want you to tell the girls tonight."

This time, she didn't fight him. This time, she didn't turn her face away. He kissed her on the cheek, and then he kissed her on the top of the head. She knew he loved the smell of her hair.

And then he was gone.

In the middle of the afternoon, Madsen went to the church to move a couple of heavy statues. Joan wanted them in different positions — he had to smile when he thought of how she'd taken over this entire parish — and he'd promised he'd tug them into the positions she wanted.

He came in the side door, and at first glance found the church was empty. He came to the center aisle, genuflected, then started to walk through the open communion rail when he heard a faint stirring in the back.

In the last pew, looking as lost as a runaway child, sat Red Carney. Just sitting there.

Madsen decided to go speak to him. He didn't need to get very close before he could smell the whiskey.

"Hello, Carney."

"Hi, Father." Looking and sounding awful. "I've been drinking again. I'm not drunk — but I've been drinking."

"Then it's a good time to pray. Before you drink any more, I mean."

"I'm sorry about the other day on the roof."

The priest smiled. "I'd say we both gave as good as we got."

"I didn't want to be up there in the first place."

Madsen nodded. "Yeah, I sort of had that impression."

"I *need* this job, Father. I've got a wife and kids to support."

"I know you do."

Carney nodded to the altar. "I don't go to Mass as regular as I should."

"You're here now. That's what matters."

Neither man spoke for a time. Then Carney said, "The funny thing is, I don't ever dream much. At least, I don't remember it much if I do. Drunk or sober, doesn't matter. No dreams. But ever since I killed Karl Schmitt —"

"A lot of people think you're a hero."

"Some hero. Come to find out he wasn't even packing a gun. His brother'd made him turn it over."

"You couldn't know that."

"The point is, Father —" Carney started to say in a loud and angry voice. A man greatly angry with himself, Madsen thought. Then, quietly: "The point is, I never should've agreed to get up on that roof and kill him."

"Robbers who take hostages always run the risk of getting killed themselves. That's just the way it is."

Carney stared up at him. "You sound like you're siding with Petty."

"No, I'm just pointing out that it's not unheard of for a lawman to kill a thief who's taken hostages. The lawman can always make the argument that he was saving more lives than he was taking. In some cases, that's pretty hard to argue with."

"In some cases. Not this one. Petty doesn't usually act that way. He always says shooting is the last resort. He likes to think he's a modern lawman, not just some gunny with a badge. And then he has me do something like this."

"Have you said any of this to Petty?"

"He'd fire me."

"You could always go to the county attorney."

Carney shook his head. "He's one of Petty's best friends. He'd get hold of Petty right away. Besides, what would I say?"

"That he should question Petty about why he ordered you to kill Schmitt when he knew that would only get some of the hostages killed — particularly Tom Rattigan."

Carney said, "I told Petty that that day. About he'd be getting Tom Rattigan killed."

"What'd he say?"

"Basically, that we had to take the chance."

"I'd mention that to the county attorney, too."

"He won't do anything about it."

"Maybe he'll surprise you."

Carney laughed sourly, expelling whiskey breath as he did so. "You're not from around here, Father. This town is a tight little club. They all take care of each other."

"You can't go on like this, Carney. You're a police officer. You can't start the day off by drinking and then come to church and sit in the back."

"I'll be all right. I just need to — stop thinking about it is all. I did it. It's over. There's nothing I can do about it. I just have to be strong is all."

"Every time you see Petty you're going to think about being up on that roof."

"I should've let you whip me. Then I wouldn't have been able to shoot him." He placed his hands on the back of the pew in front of him and levered himself up. He looked just the faintest bit whiskey-wobbly. His drinking showed more in his movements than his voice.

"Where to now?" Madsen asked.

"To be a police officer, like you said."

"You be all right?"

"I'm not drunk, if that's what you mean. I can hold the booze pretty well when I need to. Besides, most places in town won't serve me when I'm in uniform this way. Petty told them not to."

"Can't blame him for that, can you?"

"Nope. And I don't, either."

"So you'll be all right?"

"I'll have a little coffee and walk off the worst of it."

"You can always come back here and talk if you need to."

Carney watched him carefully. "You think it was cold-blooded murder, too, don't you?"

"Yeah, I guess I do."

"You don't like him, do you?" There was a drunkard for you. Less than two minutes ago he'd been accusing Madsen of taking Petty's side.

"Not much, I guess."

"I wish I could go to the county attorney, Father, but I can't. I couldn't do it to my wife and kids."

"I understand."

"You do, honestly?"

Madsen shrugged. "I don't have a wife and kids. I don't live in this town. I don't have a past with Walter Petty. So it's easy for me to tell you what to do, Carney. I don't have anything at stake. You're the one who has to make the decision. You have to weigh all those things."

"You're a good man, Father."

"So are you, Carney, though I'm not sure you see that. You're trying hard to do the right thing in difficult circumstances. I'm not sure most of us would be as brave as you are. Most of us would just walk away and forget all about it and get on with our lives. You're struggling with it. And suffering with it. That says quite a bit for you, Carney. You have strong principles."

Carney had tears in his eyes. "Thanks for saying that, Father. I needed to hear that. I really did."

Madsen said, "If you want to talk sometime, I'll be here for another day or so."

He left Carney in the last pew.

Kin of the Schmitt boys picked up the bodies at the undertaker's and loaded them on a wagon. Petty stood on the boardwalk in front of the police station watching them go. They'd stopped to see him when they first arrived in town. An old man and woman, too old to have sons the age of Karl and Leonard. They must've been in their forties when the boys were little. They were grubby, mostly silent, mournful. Dirt farmers probably. He was cold to them. If they understood this, they didn't seem to mind. They just wanted their boys was all.

At his desk once again, Petty worked on forms and composed a second letter about new weapons. In this letter he talked about how a new rifle might have helped curtail the bank robbery of a few days past. He left it to the imagination of the town council to figure out exactly *how* this would have helped. He didn't have to worry about being too specific. There was a general satisfaction with Petty now, and he knew they were going to give him his guns.

He just wished things were going as well with Caroline. She was going to do the right thing, but for the wrong reason. She was coming back to him for the sake of the children. Not because she wanted to be his wife. He sensed that she had long ago ceased wanting to be his wife. It wasn't just Tom . . . he'd lost her long before anything started with Tom. He'd just been afraid to admit it. She hadn't loved him from the start, and he'd never been able to *make* her love him. He wondered if she knew how much he loved her and how much she could hurt him. He used to see her sit up at night — again, long before Tom — staring out through a frosty winter window at the moon, and he'd sensed her mood . . . her mind and soul were apart from him, soaring to that silver disc of moon . . . dreams of another, more enriching life . . . that was what she thought of in the somber silence of three a.m. at her daydream windows. For all his arrogance — and he had no trouble admitting he was arrogant; hell, he had a number of things to be arrogant *about* — he'd never had any confidence around her, felt awkward and desperate and foolish.

Sometimes, life just didn't make any sense at all. This office, for instance. The glassed-in bookcase. The good furniture shipped recently from Chicago. The plaques and citations on the wall heralding his competence as a lawman. The photographs of him with governors and senators and rich men, including his father-in-law. These were the things he had wanted all his life. And yet they didn't satisfy him because he'd lost his wife. Tom was dead, just as he'd hoped, just as he'd planned . . .

. . . and Walt Petty *still* didn't have his wife back. And never would.

Jennings knew this was going to be a bad one. Carney was loud and silly, and whenever he started out loud and silly, it was going to be a bad one. A lot of drunkards were like that. They'd start out and it'd be like a party, laughing and slapping people on the back and ordering drinks for all their so-called friends. But there was an arc to a drunkard's drinking. Up, up, up — then down, down, down. Down in all respects. Down in coherence, down in volume, down in mood.

At least Carney had had the good sense to take off the damned uniform. He wore a work shirt and jeans. And he wasn't carrying a gun.

Maybe this would work out all right.

Jennings kept busy behind the bar, setting up beers and whiskies and water chasers, making sure that the drifters gobbling up the free eats bought at least one mug of beer an hour.

He also checked on Carney every few minutes. Carney was still in the up, up, up phase of his drunkenness, going from table to table and having himself just one hell of a good time, letting people tell him about what a good job he'd done, killing that sonofabitch Karl Schmitt, and letting them say that when Petty moved on into politics, they sure hoped that Carney became chief of police. He damn well deserved it, he did.

Up, up, up.

And so the early afternoon went.

Ellie missed two questions in Latin class that afternoon. Ellie Rattigan *never* missed questions in Latin class.

Miss Elvina Houghton looked at her sympathetically, though. Poor girl. Losing her father that way. No wonder she'd missed two questions in Latin class.

But Ellie wasn't thinking about her father. She was thinking about her mother. And her father's Civil War pistol. My God, what if Mother went insane and took the gun and went looking for Walter Petty?

Ellie stared out the window. Ellie gazed out the door into the corridor. Ellie stared at her elegant hands folded one upon the other on her desk.

And Miss Elvina Houghton understood. These were the things a proper young lady would do when she had lost her father to the kind of barbarians who — thankfully — were seeing their last days in the Old West. The New West was here, and there was no room for such people in it.

Ellie wasn't called on any more that afternoon. Miss Elvina Houghton didn't have the heart. Simply didn't have the heart. When class was over, all the students left but lovely Ellie. She was so caught up in her own thoughts, she was still in her desk.

"School's out for the day, Ellie." Miss Houghton spoke as gently as possible.

She figured Ellie Rattigan had had just about all the clamor she could handle for a long, long time to come.

Then Ellie, seemingly almost transfixed, stood, picked up her books, and walked out of the classroom, taking her deeply troubled expression with her.

FIFTEEN

They had an early supper at the rectory, after which Monsignor Gomez went to bed. He was running a slight fever, and Joan mothered him right straight to his room.

Madsen planned to spend the evening reading. Tomorrow he would get a ticket and head back home. His time here was done. Whatever happened with Rattigan and the Schmitts was beyond the ministrations of man's law.

He was reading *From Earth to the Moon* by a Frenchman named Jules Verne. Some of his priest friends thought that even contemplating traveling in space was blasphemous and challenged God's order of things. Others thought it was just silly, a waste of time and thought.

Madsen loved it. At night he used to climb up on the orphanage roof and watch the stars and wonder what they were all about. The old myths and fables about the moon and stars held no interest for him. He wanted to know about the *reality* of space. Verne at least had some serious ideas in his book. Serious and fascinating. Madsen put his feet on a footstool, his butt in a comfortable chair, turned up the reading lamp, and set about enjoying himself.

Just after dinner, one of Petty's cops was at Petty's front door. Petty said, "Come in, John."

The cop shook his head. "It's something you'd maybe better handle right away, sir."

"There's trouble?"

"Yessir." He paused. "With Carney, sir."

"Carney?" The chief sounded angry. "Now what's the problem?"

"He's over to Jennings' saloon and he's — well, he's talking about how he came to kill that Schmitt boy, sir. He's getting some of the louts who hang out there pretty worked up. Me'n the boys, we don't have no power to make him go home. But I thought you, sir — you could —"

"Thanks, John. I'll be down there shortly."

"Yessir." Pause. "Oh, and tell your wife that whatever she cooked for supper sure smells nice."

"I'll pass along the compliment. Thank you."

He moved deliberately, but not quickly enough to alarm Caroline. He went to his study, where he kept his police arms under lock and key, set his holster rig around his waist, pinned a spare badge to a leather vest. White shirt and blue trousers would be good enough. An informal call on one of his officers who was not representing the police department at all well. Ease him out of the saloon in a friendly way, then take him down by the alley and kick the living shit out of him.

He peeked into the parlor, where Caroline was playing piano with the girls. "A little business has come up. I'll be back pretty soon."

She looked at his holster. "You don't usually wear that in the evening, do you?"

"That's because evening calls are usually social ones. This one's a little more serious than that."

Her face tightened. "It's Carney, isn't it?"

"Yes," he said, "it's Carney."

Then he got out of there. He didn't want to see her gloat. Maybe she couldn't find it within herself to publicly question what he'd done — but would she be truly sorry if Carney did?

"You just get that priest down here and ask 'im," Carney was saying to the men along the bar.

Jennings, the owner, had had a lodge meeting tonight. He'd given up trying to silence Carney. Carney was one of those drunkards who expressed all his thoughts, even if they were vague, even if they were half-baked. As now. While he'd been hinting for several hours now that Walter Petty wanted one of the Schmitt boys killed for a personal reason, he'd never said what that reason was. Not that this deterred his audience of fellow drunkards from listening or offering theories of their own. One man even suggested that Chief Petty was in on the robbery himself and wanted the Schmitt boys killed before they could implicate him. It was getting crazy, and Ralph Foster, the night bartender, just stood at the far end of the bar and listened.

The thing was, Foster thought, Petty sure wasn't going to like this sort of talk. He was a proud man and a mean one.

Just then Carney reeled out the back door to vomit in the latrine. This was his third trip. Puking ended many a night for some drunkards; for others, a good vomit was completely rejuvenating. Carney was of the latter variety. He returned a few minutes later steadier and calmer.

"Beer," he said.

When Foster served him, the bartender leaned in and said, "You better keep quiet about Petty. He'll fire you, you talk like that about him."

Carney wasn't steadier or calmer after all. He said grandly, "He can't fire me. I know what happened that day."

Foster shrugged. "It's your job."

"Damn right it's my job," Carney loudly proclaimed, "and nobody's gonna take it from me, either!"

Foster rolled his eyes. At this stage, Carney was starting to sound like a stage ham.

Molly was still as a statue. Sitting in her husband's study, a lone candle guttering, casting shadows with a singularly diabolical aspect against the walls.

Tom's war gun in her right hand.

Ellie stood in the doorway. Had been there for a couple of minutes. Her mother hadn't noticed her at all.

Ellie had to make sure that her mother didn't do anything foolish. If that meant standing in this doorway all night, that was what she'd do.

Molly said, "I see you there." She kept her eyes straight ahead, not looking in Ellie's direction at all.

"Oh. I didn't think you did."

"You're thinking that I might be going to kill him."

"Have you been drinking?"

"A little."

"Mom, you know you can't drink. You always get sick."

"Not tonight. Tonight I'm too angry to get sick." She finally angled her head toward Ellie. "Your father would be alive if it wasn't for him."

"Please don't talk like that, Mother."

Molly smiled coldly. "You don't worry about me, Ellie. Don't you worry about your old mother at all."

She was very, very drunk, and Ellie wasn't quite sure what to do.

A policeman came for Madsen, a tall, angular Mexican with an eternally sad face.

Joan let the man in the front door of the rectory and brought him straight to the study, where Madsen was engrossed in his Jules Verne book.

"Carney is not too good, Father. We are afraid for him. The way he talks. The chief, he will not be happy. And Carney is very drunk, Father."

Madsen was on his feet at once, following the policeman out the door.

The thing was to stay in control of himself. No matter what Carney might have said to anybody — or implied — Petty had to seem as if his accusations meant nothing to him, as if he understood how guilty Carney felt about killing a man, and as if he wanted to help ease Carney's guilt by taking it on as his own. A lot of passing-through lawmen drank there, as well as most of his own men. He'd say in that just-folks tone he had when he wanted to show people he was just a humble, common-sensible, human man like they were, he'd say:

Killing that sonofabitch wasn't Carney's idea, it was mine. And the only reason I wanted to do it was to bring everything to a head. You know how these hostage situations are. Once those boys started shooting people, I don't have to tell you what could have happened. But Carney here . . . well, Carney here never killed a man before. And he's having a hard time dealing with it. Some men do. And that's not a mark against them, either. A lot of my men in the war were like that. They were

scared of dying, but they didn't relish the no-
tion of killing, either. So what Carney's con-
vinced himself of — and a lot of this is the
John Barleycorn playing on his mind, if you
ask me — is that we did something terrible
that morning when he shot Karl Schmitt.

Well, we didn't. And I sure didn't plan on
any of the hostages getting shot, either. What I
hoped was that since there would be only one
of them left, he'd give himself up. I think you
men know me well enough to understand that
I was just trying to bring things to a peaceful
end. That's why I've always preferred the term
peace officer to law officer. Because that's what
they taught us, to bring peace and *law to our*
towns — but peace comes first. Because you
can't have law until you have peace. So I'm
just going to take Carney here on home and
see that his wife puts him to bed. And then I'm
going to give him a few weeks off so he can
take a little vacation. Go somewhere. Get his
head cleared. And then he's welcome to come
back to work.

He actually liked to give speeches in his
head. Sometimes he could give himself ac-
tual chills, the speeches were so good. And
he knew just which voice to use. He had a
whole theater company of voices — voices
for the common man, voices for the important man, voices for just regular everyday

women, and voices for the beautiful wives of important men. All good practice for when he decided to pursue his political career.

He reached the saloon. A player piano plinked on endlessly. Laughter. The occasional slap of cards at a poker table. Shouts for more beer at the tables. If Carney was holding court, it was to a damned small audience. And he was having to shout above one whole hell of a lot of noise.

Petty went up the three steps to the porch, walked to the bat-wings, pushed on in. Smoke and noise slapped him across the face. He wanted to back right out, into the clean night air. Everything looked as he'd expected it — most of the tables taken up with poker, a couple of buxom saloon gals serving drinks and getting pinched-poked-prodded over virtually every inch of their bodies, and a long line of men with their backs to him along the bar. Rochester lamps hanging low over every table.

Carney was at the end of the bar. His disciples were small in number. Probably he'd had a much bigger audience earlier. But like most drunkards, Carney tended to repeat himself and ramble on into incoherence. The four or five men who stood listening to him now swayed and tottered as much as he did. A drunk speaking to other drunks. This wasn't going to be difficult at all.

As he approached Carney's back, the small group of listeners looked up and saw Petty. Three of them nodded toward him, obviously hoping to silence Carney.

But he went drunkenly on. "*He* didn't have nerve enough to kill the son of a bitch, so he had me do it. The way I'm always doin' his dirty work for him. Remember Jake Forrester, got sent up for stealing Old Man Skinner's saddle? I planted that saddle because that's what Skinner asked Petty to do. Those two are thick as thieves."

It was odd. Petty had come in here fearing that he might hear something about Karl Schmitt that would really put him in some trouble. He hadn't even thought of the other things, the infractions of law that Carney might just be able to *prove* — all those bits and pieces of dirty work that had resulted in a number of men being put in prison. Nobody got hanged; nobody served life. But certain influential people around town had wanted — for various reasons — certain *un*influential people removed from town, and Petty, as the protector of the high-and-mighty, Petty had felt obligated to oblige. So he'd had Carney — who was always on the brink of being fired for his drinking and couldn't afford to say no — do the dirty work for him.

Now Carney was talking about this work in a loud if slurred voice to anybody who wanted to hear.

One of Petty's men, drunk but not drunk enough to not grasp the situation here, said, "You better turn around, Carney."

"Turn aroun'?"

"And see who's behind you?"

"Who's behind —"

"No need for that," Petty said amiably. "I will walk around myself."

And so he did.

Carney, strangely, didn't seem to have any reaction at all when seeing Petty. Maybe he was so drunk he didn't recognize him at first.

But then he drew himself up and without warning, spat in Petty's face.

It was too much to say that everything came to a halt. The player piano still played, the saloon gals still sashayed themselves across the barroom floor, and the man behind the bar still poured drinks.

But for approximately one third of the men in the saloon, none of the background mattered anymore. They were all staring at the drama at the end of the bar. And since a good number of them were policemen, they had a special interest in what was happening. They had all longed to do just what Carney had done to the imperious Petty — spit in his fucking face.

Now they waited to see how Petty would respond.

He took out his handkerchief and wiped away the spittle. Then he noticed the gun Carney was holding.

Somebody stopped the player piano. The poker games ceased. The saloon girls collected behind the bar. Foster brought up the sawed-off.

Carney said, "You can kill me, Foster. But Petty goes before I do."

Petty, very much in control of himself, said, "Red, put that fucking gun of yours away. This is crazy. What's your wife going to say?"

"Right now, I don't give a shit what anybody says."

"That's because you're drunk."

"I don't want any more lectures from you, Petty. I'm sick of you and all your bullshit. All the things you made me do over the years. Why, if I told people — we'd *both* be in prison and you know it.

And then I had to kill that Schmitt boy on top of everything. Because *you* made me. You didn't even give a damn about your so-called friend Tom Rattigan, did you?"

The thing was to shut Carney up before he said anything more. And again, not about the bank robbery, but about illegal things Carney had done for him over the years. "Give me your gun, Red, and we'll go drink some coffee and have a nice little talk."

"C'mon, Red," said a man behind him.

"Yeah, Red, we don't want to see nothin' happen to ya," said another.

Red Carney was liked. No doubt about it. He was a genuinely decent man when he was sober.

Petty decided this was a good time to take a few steps forward and see if he could ease the gun out of Carney's hand. "C'mon now, Red."

Carney startled everybody by firing into the floor just beside Petty's boot.

"No more of your bullshit, Walt. You're never gonna slick-talk me — or blackmail me into doing what you want — ever again."

The situation was worse than Petty had originally surmised. He could deal with it, but it was going to take a little more skill and patience than he'd originally counted on.

"Somebody go get his wife," Petty said softly. "Bring her down here."

"No!" Carney said. "This is between you and me. Leave my wife out of it!"

Petty shook his head at the man who'd been going for the wife. "If he doesn't want her here, let's just forget it." Then, to Carney, knowing that the direct way was the best way to deal with this moment, he said, "Where you going to put the bullet, Red?" He touched the center of his forehead. "This is a good spot. Or maybe here." And he touched his heart. "Or here." And he touched his eye. "But you might put a little thought to the swamper who'll have to clean up the mess. You don't want to make it too tough on him."

"You're trying to talk me down, aren't you, Petty? You forget, I've seen all the bullshit you pull on people. You can talk people into goin' crazy. But it won't work on me. Because I'm gonna kill you, Petty. Right here and right now. And Foster can blast with me that sawed-off of his and I don't give a shit. Because that's where I am in my life, Petty. *I don't give a shit.* And when a man don't give a shit, he's the most dangerous man around."

And with that, Carney raised the gun and trained it on Petty's chest.

Madsen came through the bat-wings. Civilian clothes. Wouldn't know he was a priest.

It was like walking onto a theater stage. All the actors frozen in place for the big showdown scene. He walked among the actors as if they were statues, and went right up to Carney.

"This doesn't make a lot of sense, Red," Madsen said. "You're mad at Petty for making you kill a man — and yet you're willing to kill Petty."

"Another talker," Carney scoffed. "I'm sorry, Father. But I'd just as soon you turned around and headed back to your little church and left me the hell alone."

"Think about your family, Red."

Carney laughed. "You're a little late with that one, Father. Petty here beat you to it. He also offered to buy me a cup of coffee and work things out. And Foster there's gonna put a hole in my middle as soon as I pull the trigger. They've tried pretty much everything, Father. Nothing personal — I actually like you — but I'm gonna kill him and there's nobody gonna stop me." He angled his head a moment and said, "And if you're wondering why nobody's jumped me from behind, it's because they know no matter how fast they can grab me, I can kill him first."

"He isn't going to kill me," Petty said to Madsen. "If he was going to, he would've done it by now. He wants to try and humiliate me. That's what he's really after here. He wants to show people that I'm afraid of having a gun held on me." He looked around at the men in the saloon. "Well, hell, yes, I am. Who wouldn't be? But what does that prove? That I'm just like everybody else? So what?" He dared a half step. Carney raised the gun to Petty's face. "Red, I'm asking you before this business gets any crazier, let's let you and me go and drink some coffee and talk this through."

"Listen to him, Red," Madsen said. "That's a very good idea. Talking it through isn't going to hurt you."

"I'm sick of talk," Carney said. Then: "You know what he's afraid of? That I'll tell everybody exactly which cases we trumped up to put certain people in prison. *That's* what he's afraid of here."

Petty had begun his calculation. He had decided that Carney really was going to kill him and that the only way he could extricate himself from that fate was to dive under Carney's gun and throw Carney to the floor. He might still be killed, but at this point he had no other choice.

Madsen said, "Red, why don't you give me your gun?"

"You on his side now, Father?"

"Red, I just want your gun before it's too late."

"I should've figured it. Petty got to you, too, didn't he, Father? The way he gets to everybody. Well, I'll tell you one thing, he ain't gettin' to me anymore. That's for sure."

The hammer eased back on the gun. A sorrow filled Red Carney's gaze. His finger trembled on the trigger.

Petty made his move. Dove under the gun, which exploded with a shot the moment his arms grappled around Carney's waist.

There was a ten-foot space between the end of the bar and the wall. Carney was knocked flat and went skidding across the floor, slamming into the wall, losing his grip on his gun as he did so.

Madsen was there before everybody else. He had the gun in his hand and waved it around with great authority. "Barkeep, you get Carney up on his feet and start pouring black coffee down him. You other men go back to what you were doing before all this started. Somebody run and get Carney's wife and have her come down here. I'll help her get him home."

The men were surprisingly obedient. They wanted the old routine back as quickly as they could get it. For all the violence of the Old West, there weren't many men who had much stomach for bloodshed. It was usually unnecessary and always scary. Let the Hickocks and the Earp brothers and the James boys build their reputations. Their lives were generally short-lived.

"You have any orders for me?" Petty said sardonically. "Seeing as how you're taking over our little town, Father." A tic in his right eye revealed that fear had aftereffects.

The noise was such that they could stand at the bar and not worry about being overheard. The damned player piano could make a man deaf.

Madsen drank a beer. Petty had a shot of rye.

Madsen said, "You had your friend Tom Rattigan killed. And you had poor Carney do it for you. Nothing's ever going to come of it because nobody can ever prove it."

"You're right, Padre," Petty said, throwing back his shot, "nobody can ever prove it."

"You'll keep on being police chief here for a while, until you decide to make your move politically. And who knows, you might even become governor."

"All the way to Washington, D.C., is how I have it planned." Petty smiled. "I'm not a humble man, Father."

Madsen stared at him. "And you may get away with it. Never have to face what you had Carney do for you. Or what you did to Tom Rattigan or those poor stupid Schmitt boys."

"They were criminals."

"Criminals, yes, but not killers."

"They could've been."

"Possibly. But you didn't know that when you ordered Carney to kill one of them." Madsen wiped off his beer mustache. "I believe there's a life after this one, Petty. It may take all that time, but there's somebody you'll have to face for what you did. You won't have any choice."

Petty sighed. "I'm sort of tired now, Padre. I hope you won't mind if I go home to my wife and family now. Plus, I don't think I can take any more of his crying."

Red Carney had his head down on the table and was sobbing. Foster was offering him coffee, but to no avail.

"Good night, Father. Give my best to the

monsignor." Petty gave him a jaunty salute and walked toward the bat-wings.

"Another beer, Father?" Foster said.

"Thanks," Madsen said.

Foster brought him a fresh one and said, "Poor old Red. He's gonna have one hell of a hangover tomorrow. And no job."

The gunshot sounded, then. And almost instantly afterward, a second, then a third gunshot. Stark and clear and loud even above the din of the saloon.

Men rushed to the bat-wings. Much as they might detest violence, they were drawn to the witnessing of it. Watching violence was the male equivalent of gossip. It was shameful, but irresistible.

Madsen was a few seconds late getting to the street.

The streetlamps weren't much help. He saw a circle of men. There was talk, but nothing he could decipher from here. He trotted over to where they stood at the mouth of an alley. He worked his way through the crowd.

Petty lay facedown, unmoving. Madsen knelt down, checked neck and wrist for pulse. None. Three bloody holes in his back.

"Anybody see who did this?" Madsen said.

"No, Father."

"Alley was empty when I ran back there."

"Sonofabitch got clean away."

Madsen stood up. "Somebody better run for the doc and the undertaker. And whoever's in charge after Petty and Carney better take over now."

The police officers who'd been drinking and pokering away their off hours nodded and set to work.

Madsen drifted away from the crowd to the alley, a place narrow and dark now that heavy rain clouds hid the half-moon.

Merchants had lined the alley with crates and boxes of various sorts. The lane smelled of dust and oil from the wagon works and heat from the day. Two or three kittens romped about. When the moon did come through, it cast long, lonely shadows across the backs of buildings. Madsen walked up and down the alley several times, peering inside several containers, finding nothing.

Sonofabitch got clean away seemed to have said it all.

Then he saw the small black-and-white kitten pawing at a large crate with the end flap slightly ajar. The kitten was trying to open the flap wider so it could get inside. Something in there was important to the kitten. Madsen wondered if it would also prove to be important to him.

This crate was behind another one. He'd missed it. He moved the front crate away, and then reached over and opened the flap.

There was a girl in there, huddled in the back. Her gentle, lovely eyes showed great fear. She was crying silently and trembling terribly.

He reached in. The gun looked far too big for her small hand. It was like coaxing an injured wild bird from a hiding hole. You had to first somehow convince it you meant it no harm.

When she finally came out, her legs were wobbly. She stood in the moonlight, where he could see the port-wine stain that covered the left side of her face.

SIXTEEN

The train came at 3:07 the following afternoon. Joan and the monsignor stood with Madsen on the platform. Only one other man, a farmer, was boarding. The day was hot and windy, and blown sand kept people nursing their eyes.

"That poor family," Joan was saying. "First they lose their father, and now the young girl will be put away somewhere." She looked at them both and said, "I know you don't want to hear this, but sometimes it's hard to believe in any kind of God at all."

The old monsignor smiled sadly. "Whole months go by when I do not believe in Him, after He's let something terrible happen. God's wisdom is beyond us is all I can tell you. Sometimes it's a wisdom that makes me very, very angry. I suppose that's why Job is my favorite part of the Bible. He alone has the nerve to speak up to God and demand an explanation for it all."

"Well, now," Joan said, "a priest who tells the truth — at last."

"My optimism irritates her sometimes," Madsen said. "She's always telling me that I should be a lot gloomier than I am." Then he laughed, and she came into his arms, half-lover, half-daughter. They hugged each other for a long time. In the days ahead they would drift apart, promised letters fewer and fewer over the years, Madsen old and then Madsen dead, and Joan on to whatever life the years ahead held for her. This was not a temporary good-bye, but a permanent one.

Then he was stepping on the train and waving good-bye. He took the seat near the back of the Pullman, where the noise would be slightly less. He was much more dispirited than he let on, and about everything. *Sometimes it's a wisdom that makes me very, very angry,* the old monsignor had said.

But Father Madsen didn't want to think about that now. His days here had been too damned sad. He just wanted to forget it all.

He opened his Jules Verne *From Earth to the Moon* and began reading. Sometimes the moon was a good place to be.